# Anna and the Swallow Man

Kraków, 1939.
A million marching soldiers and a thousand barking dogs.
This is no place to grow up.

Anna Łania is just seven years old when the Germans take
her father, and suddenly, she's alone. Then she meets The
Swallow Man. He is a mystery, strange and tall, and like
Anna's missing father, he has a gift for languages: Polish,
Russian, German, Yiddish – even Bird. When he calls
a bright, beautiful swallow down to his hand to stop her
from crying, Anna is entranced.

Over the course of their travels together, Anna and the
Swallow Man will dodge bombs, tame soldiers and even,
despite their better judgment, make a friend. But in a world
gone mad, everything can prove dangerous . . .

**Gavriel Savit** is an actor as well as a writer.
He lives in New York.
You can find him at
www.gavrielsavit.com
@GavrielSavit

# Anna and the Swallow Man

GAVRIEL SAVIT

THE BODLEY HEAD
LONDON

**ANNA AND THE SWALLOW MAN**
A BODLEY HEAD BOOK
Hardback: 978 1 782 30052 6
Trade paperback: 978 1 782 30053 3

First published in Great Britain by The Bodley Head,
an imprint of Random House Children's Publishers UK
A Penguin Random House Company

This edition published 2016

1 3 5 7 9 10 8 6 4 2

Text copyright © Gavriel Savit, 2016
Cover and interior illustrations © Laura Carlin, 2016

Penguin Random House is committed to a sustainable future for our business, our readers
and our planet. This book is made from Forest Stewardship Council® certified paper.

Published by Random House Children's Publishers UK
61–63 Uxbridge Road, London W5 5SA

www.randomhousechildrens.co.uk
www.randomhouse.co.uk

Addresses for companies within The Random House Group Limited
can be found at: www.randomhouse.co.uk/offices.htm

THE RANDOM HOUSE GROUP Limited Reg. No. 954009

A CIP catalogue record for this book is available from the British Library.

Printed and bound in Great Britain by Clays Ltd, St Ives plc

*For Sophie "Sunnie" Tait,*
*of blessed memory,*
*as a poor return for all the wonderful*
*books she gave me*

# What Do You Say?

When Anna Łania woke on the morning of the sixth of November in the year 1939—her seventh—there were several things that she did not know:

Anna did not know that the chief of the Gestapo in occupied Poland had by fiat compelled the rector of the Jagiellonian University to require the attendance of all professors (of whom her father was one) at a lecture and discussion on the direction of the Polish Academy under German sovereignty, to take place at noon on that day.

She did not know that, in the company of his colleagues, her father would be taken from lecture hall number 56, first to a prison in Kraków, where they lived, and subsequently to a number of other internment facilities across Poland, before finally being transported to the Sachsenhausen concentration camp in Germany.

She also did not know that, several months later, a group

of her father's surviving colleagues would be moved to the far more infamous Dachau camp in Upper Bavaria, but that, by the time of that transfer, her father would no longer exist in a state in which he was capable of being moved.

What Anna did know that morning was that her father had to go away for a few hours.

Seven-year-old girls are a hugely varied bunch. Some of them will tell you that they've long since grown up, and you'd have trouble not agreeing with them; others seem to care much more about the hidden childhood secrets chalked on the insides of their heads than they do about telling a grown-up anything at all; and still others (this being the largest group by far) have not yet entirely decided to which camp they belong, and depending on the day, the hour, even the moment, they may show you completely different faces from the ones you thought you might find.

Anna was one of these last girls at age seven, and her father helped to foster the ambivalent condition. He treated her like an adult—with respect, deference, and consideration—but somehow, simultaneously, he managed to protect and preserve in her the feeling that everything she encountered in the world was a brand-new discovery, unique to her own mind.

Anna's father was a professor of linguistics at the Jagiellonian University in Kraków, and living with him meant that every day of the week was in a different language. By the time Anna had reached the age of seven, her German, Russian, French, and English were all good, and she had a fair amount of Yiddish and Ukrainian and a little Armenian and Carpathian Romany as well.

Her father never spoke to her in Polish. The Polish, he said, would take care of itself.

One does not learn as many languages as Anna's father had without a fair bit of love for talking. Most of her memories of her father were of him speaking—laughing and joking, arguing and sighing—with one of the many friends and conversation partners he cultivated around the city. In fact, for much of her life with him, Anna had thought that each of the languages her father spoke had been tailored, like a bespoke suit of clothes, to the individual person with whom he conversed. French was not French; it was Monsieur Bouchard. Yiddish was not Yiddish; it was Reb Shmulik. Every word and phrase of Armenian that Anna had ever heard reminded her of the face of the little old *tatik* who always greeted her and her father with small cups of strong, bitter coffee.

Every word of Armenian smelled like coffee.

If Anna's young life had been a house, the men and women with whom her father spent his free time in discourse would've been its pillars. They kept the sky up and the earth down, and they smiled and spoke to her as if she were one of their own children. It was never only Professor Łania coming to visit them; it was Professor Łania and Anna. Or, as they might have it, Professor Łania and Anja, or Khannaleh, or Anke, or Anushka, or Anouk. She had as many names as there were languages, as there were people in the world.

Of course, if each language is for only one person, then eventually a girl begins to wonder, *What is my father's language? What is mine?*

But the answer was quite simple—they were speakers of other people's languages. Everyone else seemed tied down to only one, at best to two or three, but Anna's father seemed to be entirely unbound by the borders that held everyone else in the wide and varied landscape of Kraków. He was not confined to any one way of speaking. He could be anything he wanted. Except, perhaps, himself.

And if this was true of Anna's father, well, then it must have been true for Anna, too. Instead of passing on to his daughter one particular language that would define her, Anna's father gave her the wide spectrum of tongues that he knew, and said, "Choose amongst them. Make something new for yourself."

In none of her memories of him was Anna's father not saying something. He lived, in her memory, like a vibrant statue, molded in the shape of his accustomed listening posture: right knee bent over the left, elbow propped against the knee, his chin in his palm. He adopted this attitude frequently, but even when so silently bound in attention, Anna's father couldn't help but communicate, and his lips and eyebrows would wriggle and squirm in reaction to the things people said to him. Other people would have to ask him what these idiosyncratic tics and twitches meant, but Anna was fluent in that language, too, and she never had to ask.

She and her father spent so very much time talking together. They talked in every language in every corner of their apartment, and all throughout the streets of the city. Of all people, she was certain that he liked talking to her best.

The first time Anna realized that a language was a com-

4

promise shared amongst people—that two people who spoke the same language were not necessarily the same—this was the only time she could remember asking her father a question that he could not manage to answer.

They had been making their way home from some outing or other, and it had been growing dark. Anna didn't recognize the part of the city where they were walking. Her father was holding on to her hand very tightly, and his long-legged strides forced her to trot to keep up. His pace quickened, faster and faster as the sun dipped beneath the rooftops and then the hills beyond, and by the time it happened, they were practically running.

She heard them before she saw anything. There was a man's voice laughing, loud and jolly, so genuinely amused that Anna began smiling as well, excited to see whatever it was that was making the laughter. But when they arrived at the street from which the sound was coming, her smiling stopped.

There were three soldiers.

The laughing soldier was the smallest. She didn't remember the two others very clearly, except that they seemed impossibly large to her.

"Jump!" said the smallest soldier. "Jump! Jump!"

The grizzled old man in front of them did his best to follow this direction, hopping up and down pointlessly in place, but there was very clearly something wrong with his leg—a bad break, perhaps. It was plain to see that he was in terrible discomfort. At great expense of effort, he kept his voice silent each time his shoes hit the cobblestones, despite the pain that twisted his expression.

This seemed to delight the small soldier even more.

Perhaps the most difficult part of this memory was the pure and unreserved delight of that laughter. In Anna's mind, the soldier was speaking—and, for that matter, laughing—in Herr Doktor Fuchsmann's language.

Herr Doktor Fuchsmann was a fat, nearly bald man who always wore a waistcoat. He had spectacles and a cane, which he used to help him shuffle around his small pharmacy all day long. Herr Doktor Fuchsmann was a man who giggled, and whose face was almost always turning red. In the short time that Anna had known him, he had snuck her more cookies than she had ever even seen in any other setting.

And the small soldier was speaking Herr Doktor Fuchsmann.

Anna was confused. She could understand neither the soldier in the context of the doctor, nor the doctor in the context of the soldier. So she did what any child would do in such a situation.

She asked her father.

If Anna's father had not been the man that he was, and if Anna had not been hearing and speaking and thinking, in part, in German for as many of her seven years as had the potential for speech in them—in short, if her accent had not been so compellingly native—this story might've ended before it began.

"Papa," said Anna. "Why are they laughing at that man?"

Anna's father didn't answer. The soldier turned his head.

"Because, *Liebling*," he said. "That is not a man. That is a *Jude*."

Anna remembered that word exactly, because it changed

everything for her. She thought she knew what language was, how it worked, how people pulled in different words out of the air into which they had spoken in order to shape their outlines around them.

But this was much more complicated.

Reb Shmulik didn't say *Jude*. Reb Shmulik said *yid*.

And this soldier, no matter what language he was speaking, was as different from Herr Doktor Fuchsmann as he wanted everyone to know that he was from Reb Shmulik the Jew.

In 1939 a group of people called Germans came into a land called Poland and took control of the city Kraków, where Anna lived. Shortly thereafter these Germans instituted an operation entitled Sonderaktion Krakau, which was aimed at the intellectuals and academics of the city, of whom Anna's father was one.

The day appointed for the execution of Sonderaktion Krakau was November the sixth, 1939—Anna's seventh year—and all Anna knew that morning was that her father had to go away for a few hours.

He left her in the care of Herr Doktor Fuchsmann shortly after eleven o'clock, and then he did not come back again.

It was not uncommon for Anna's father to leave her with his friends when he had some pressing business to attend to. He trusted her enough to leave her alone in the apartment for brief periods, but on occasion, of course, he needed to be gone for longer. She was still very young, and from time to time someone was needed to look after her.

Anna's father had done his best to insulate her from what had been going on in the city, but a war is a war, and it is impossible to protect a child from the world forever. There were uniforms in the street, and people yelling, and dogs, and fear, and sometimes there were gunshots, and if a man loves to speak, eventually his daughter will hear the word "war" spoken, furtively, aloud. "War" is a heavy word in every language.

Anna remembered vaguely that there had been a time before this heavy word had descended on every side of her like the weighted edges of a net, but more than the figure or face of any particular person—more even than the brief impression she had managed to form of her mother—what principally characterized her memory of that time was the vibrant outdoor life of an exuberant city: chatting strolls in public parks and gardens; glasses of beer, or cups of coffee or tea, at tables on the sidewalk; mothers and lovers and friends calling names out across reverberant stone streets, hoping to catch and turn a beloved head before it disappeared around a corner. Those had seemed like days of perpetual warmth and sun to Anna, but war, she learned, was very much like weather—if it was on its way, it was best not to be caught outdoors.

In his final months Anna's father spent quite a bit of time inside with her, talking and, when the inevitable need for silence arose, reading. He meant very well, but most of the books he had in the house were still far beyond Anna's level, and so she spent much of her time with one particular book, a thick volume of children's stories drawn from every source. Whether they were from Aesop or the Bible, or Norse myth or Egyptian, they were all illustrated in the same comforting nineteenth-century hand, with pen and ink, reproduced there on thick, heavy paper.

Anna missed that book as soon as she was separated from it. Even before she missed her father.

For the first two or three hours after noon on the sixth of November, Herr Doktor Fuchsmann acted just as he always had toward Anna, teasing and laughing over his spectacles while the shop was empty, and immediately ignoring her as soon as the bell on the door rang a new customer inside. There were many fewer cookies now than there had been in past days, but Anna understood—Herr Doktor Fuchsmann had explained the dearth with reference to the war. This was a common practice, one with which Anna had already become quite familiar—whenever someone remarked something out of the ordinary lately, it seemed to be explained by pointing out the war.

Anna still was not certain what precisely was meant by this word "war," but it seemed, at least in part, to be an assault on her cookie supply, and of this she simply could not approve.

The shop was much busier that day than Anna had ever seen it before, and the people who came in after Herr Doktor Fuchsmann's relief seemed mostly to be young Germans in subtly differing uniforms. Even some of the older men in suits came in speaking a bright, clipped-sounding German that, though clearly the same language as the Herr Doktor's, seemed to Anna to lean forward with tight muscles, where his sat back, relaxed. It was all terribly interesting, but Herr Doktor

Fuchsmann became nervous when she paid too obvious attention to anything his customers had to say, and so she did her best to look as if she weren't listening.

He tried to mask his growing anxiety as the day drew on, but when the time came to close down his shop and Anna's father had still not returned to collect her, Herr Doktor Fuchsmann began to worry very openly.

Anna was not yet terribly worried, though. Her father had been gone for longer before, and he had always returned.

But now there were gunshots in the streets from time to time, and dogs barking constantly. Herr Doktor Fuchsmann flatly refused to take Anna home with him, and this was the first seed of worry in her. He had always been so sweet to her before, and it was confusing that he should suddenly turn unkind.

Anna slept that night beneath the counter of Herr Doktor Fuchsmann's shop, cold without a blanket, afraid to be seen or to make too much noise as the streets filled up with German in the growing night.

She had trouble falling asleep. Her worry kept her mind just active enough to prevent her from nodding off, but not quite so active that she could stop herself from growing bored. It was in this never-ending threshold of a moment that she missed her book of tales.

There was a story near its back, a story at which the cracked binding had grown accustomed to falling open, of a spindly wraith called the Alder King. Anna loved to stare at his picture until her fright reached a nearly unbearable height and then to shut it away. The fright disappeared reliably with the Alder King, trapped there between the pages of his book, and she longed to shut up her gnawing worry with him now.

In the morning Herr Doktor Fuchsmann brought Anna a little food. It comforted her, but by lunchtime it became clear that he meant not to keep her around. He was very apologetic, telling Anna that he would send her father straight along if he came back to the shop for her, but that he just couldn't have her in his shop anymore.

Everything he said made sense. Who was she to argue?

Herr Doktor Fuchsmann locked the door behind him when they left to walk Anna to her apartment. There it quickly became apparent to her that her father had locked his own door when they had left for Herr Doktor Fuchsmann's the day before. Herr Doktor Fuchsmann never learned this, though—as soon as they were within sight of the apartment building, he excused himself and hurried back to his shop.

Anna sat in front of the door to her apartment for a very long time. There was still a part of her that was sure that her father was on his way back to her, and she tried as best she could to prune her worry and encourage this certainty to grow in its place. Surely, he would be back soon.

But he did not come.

Whenever she felt her surety fading, Anna tried the apartment doorknob. Over and over she tried it, each time becoming slowly, thoroughly convinced that, in fact, her father had not locked her out, but that she had simply not turned the knob hard enough.

As much as she wanted it to be true, though, the door never budged. In days of peace, sometimes such fancies can prove true. Never, though, in times of war.

It felt like an eternity to Anna, sitting there, and in a sense it was. To a child, an empty hour is a lifetime. Anna sat there for at least two or three, and if it hadn't been for old Mrs. Niemczyk across the hall, she might've sat there waiting for her father until the war stopped her.

Mrs. Niemczyk frequently complained to Professor Łania (and others) that he and his girl spoke too loudly too late at night, but Anna's father had been convinced that she simply didn't like their bringing Gypsies and Armenians and Jews into the building. Mrs. Niemczyk spoke only Polish, and only very little of it at any one time. In all her life she had never spoken one word directly to Anna, though the old lady had frequently spoken of her to her father in her presence, usually to tell him how he was failing to bring his daughter up properly. Needless to say, she was never a particularly happy sight to Anna, and Anna was a girl who was rather well disposed to meeting people.

Shortly after Anna began her wait in front of the apartment door, Mrs. Niemczyk left her apartment briefly to run an errand. Her eyes lingered on Anna as she passed down the hall, and upon her return they didn't move from Anna once until she shut the door of her apartment behind her.

Anna wasn't sure what she thought Mrs. Niemczyk would do, but the old lady began cracking her door open every so often to check and see if the little girl was still sitting in the hall, and every time Anna saw her, what little of Mrs. Niemczyk's face she could see behind the door looked somehow better and better pleased.

If it hadn't been for old Mrs. Niemczyk, Anna might very well have stayed to wait for her father.

If it hadn't been for old Mrs. Niemczyk, Anna might very well never have met the Swallow Man.

There were scores of apartments and rooms, even cafés and taverns, across Kraków where Anna would've been welcomed in any number of languages for a day or two by one of her father's scattered friends, but still, she made her way back to Herr Doktor Fuchsmann's shop. After all, this was the last place she had seen her father. This was where he thought her to be.

It was getting later. Anna was hungry, and as the sun began its descent toward the horizon, she began wondering where she would sleep that night. It was a new feeling to her, that worry—up until the night before, the only place she'd ever slept in her life had been the little bed behind the locked door of her apartment, just down the hall from her father.

Herr Doktor Fuchsmann was busy with a customer when Anna arrived in the street outside his shop. She could see him through the big plate-glass windows, talking to a man in a suit, and though he looked directly out at her, he did not seem to see her.

It was cold there in the street.

Though she was in many ways accustomed to comporting

herself like an adult even at her age, Anna was, in those days, never short of the most childlike obedience. Herr Doktor Fuchsmann had told her he couldn't have her in his shop; no matter how sure she was that the circumstances were different from what he had thought, no matter how desperate she became, she wouldn't go in unless she was told that it was all right.

This was what adults called "being a good girl."

Anna settled down on the street to wait for a father who would not come. The street that held Herr Doktor Fuchsmann's shop was short—a curving, cobbled way, and narrow, that connected two major thoroughfares and continued beyond neither. There wasn't a lot of traffic there, and aside from those customers who came to the pharmacy and the few other shops on the ground level, most of the people that came or went from the little street lived up above it and did not linger as they arrived or departed. Anna kept her eyes down, silently pleading with each passing person not to see her, or else to be her father. She passed the time by fidgeting and seeking out what loose threads her skirt could offer for pulling.

It was the sound of shoes that finally caught her attention. The *klak-klak* rhythm must've gone up and down the street a hundred times that afternoon, circling around, back and forth, disappearing for a while and then returning again, before the sound of his wooden heel blocks against the stones of the street finally became familiar to her. When she raised her head in surprise, it was in the certainty that she knew those shoes. It wasn't long after she did that the man above the shoes noticed her noticing him.

The man was tall and exceedingly thin. His suit, brown wool and in three pieces, must've been made specifically for him. It was difficult to imagine any other man with such measurements, and his clothes fit him closer than a glove. He carried an old physician's bag, the brown leather worn a bit lighter than the color of his dark suit. It had brass fittings, and on the side of the bag was the monogram *SWG* in a faded red that must've originally been the color of his dark necktie. A tall black umbrella rode between the two handles of the bag, stacked on its top, despite the clearness of the sky.

The thin man stopped when he noticed Anna looking at him, and he looked back down at her from a terrible height through his round, gold-rimmed spectacles. There was an unlit cigarette in his mouth, which he took between his long, spindly fingers and removed, breathing in to speak.

At precisely that moment, the bell rang a young German soldier out of Herr Doktor Fuchsmann's shop and into the street. The thin man turned his head sharply to the young soldier and addressed him in bright, crisp, supremely lettered German, asking him if this was the famous doctor's establishment that everyone seemed to like so much. Anna found that she had been holding her breath.

The tall man and the stranger spoke briefly, congenially, the soldier vouching for the quality and eagerness of the service within. After all, the physician was German, and you could hardly expect one of these *Polish* doctors to rival him.

After an appropriate pause the thin man nodded his thanks to the soldier and turned his eyes toward the shop. He had an air of authority about him, and Anna began to wonder, as the soldier must've, if she ought to know who he was. The young soldier, well used to the customs of the implicit superior, interpreted the nod of curt thanks as the dismissal it was intended to be, but before he'd gotten very far off, the thin man called him back again.

"I wonder, *Soldat*," he said, "if you might light my cigarette." The thin man's long hands were clasped behind his back. There was no question at all that he might be troubled to light the thing himself.

The young soldier dutifully complied. The thin man made no eye contact and offered no word of thanks, or even of acknowledgment.

He took a long drag on his cigarette.

The soldier disappeared out into Kraków.

The thin man took another chestful of smoke before turning back to Anna.

"So," he said in his fine German, as much smoke as sound escaping his lips. "Who are you?"

Anna had no idea how to answer this question. Her jaw worked, trying to find some word in any language to sculpt out of the air—she knew that there was a version of "Anna" that the Germans used for her, but it felt somehow wrong to say to this stern authority of a man that that word was who she *was*. She was, just as much, cold, and hungry, and frightened, and her mind labored to recall which particular diminutive it was in the first place.

The thin man raised an eyebrow and cocked his head to the

right. He frowned and switched to Polish. "For whom are you waiting?"

Where his German had been bright and crisp, his Polish was just as round and swift. He was the first person Anna had heard since her father who had an equal command of more than one language.

She wanted to answer him, wanted to talk, but she didn't know what she could tell him. It occurred to her to say that she was waiting for her father, but, in point of fact, she was not so sure of the truth of this anymore, and if one thing was clear about this tall stranger, it was that he was not someone to whom one offered a lie.

The thin man nodded in answer to Anna's silence and switched to Russian. "Where are your parents?"

This question should've been easy to answer, except that Anna honestly couldn't say because she didn't know. She was about to tell him so, but by this point the tall man had grown used to her unresponsiveness and he cycled rapidly and spoke again: Yiddish.

"Are you all right?"

It was this question that made Anna cry. Of course, in their way, the others and their answerlessnesses were just as confounding, just as troubling. Perhaps it was the sudden softening of his tone—him, a man who was more than a little frightening to her then, towering up there above her, suddenly concerned. Things had been getting progressively less all right for weeks and months now, and she couldn't remember anyone else ever having asked how she was. Even her father had been so busy laboring to provide an acceptable sort of all-rightness for her that he had neglected ever to ask if it had worked.

Perhaps it was the Yiddish. That was Reb Shmulik's language. Anna had not seen Reb Shmulik in many weeks, and though she was a child, she was not blind to what was happening to the Jews of the city. Part of her had been unsure that Yiddish still survived at all until the thin man had spoken it.

The most likely explanation for Anna's tears, though, was that this was the one question that, with certainty, she knew the answer to:

She was not all right.

The thin man seemed more puzzled than concerned by her tears. Again his brows bunched together, and he cocked his head to the side as he looked down at her. As much as anything, the thin man seemed curious.

The man's eyes were very sharp. They were deep-set in his head, and even if a girl was working very hard to hide her tears from the world, she would have quite a time of trying not to watch them. Like fishhooks, his eyes captured Anna's and drew them in to him.

The next thing he did changed Anna's life forever.

The thin man turned his sharp eyes up toward the eaves of the buildings that huddled around the short street. Anna's captive gaze followed close behind. Spotting what he wanted, the thin man brought his lips close in together and spoke a chirruping, bright whistle of a phrase up in the direction of the sky.

There was a sudden noise of wings, and a bird came plummeting down to the street like a falling bomb. It spread its wings to gather in the air and slow its descent, alighted on a small gray paving stone, hopped, blinked, and cocked its head to the side, looking up at the thin man.

He passed his cigarette from his left hand to his right, and crouching down to street level, his peaked knees reaching nearly to the height of his ears, the tall man proffered his left forefinger, pointing right, parallel to the ground.

For a moment the bird was still. The thin man spoke to it again, and as if called by name, it flitted up to perch on the branch of his finger.

He turned slowly, carrying the bird over to Anna, looked her straight in her wide eyes, and raised his right forefinger to his lips in hush.

It was unnecessary. Wary of frightening the beautiful, delicate little creature, Anna had not only already stopped her crying, but again found that she was holding her breath.

Anna could see the creature incredibly clearly where he held it out to her, just inches from her face. Its head and wings were a bright, vibrant, iridescent blue, and its face and ruff were pale orange. Its tail was split in a wide fork, and it moved in quick bursts, otherwise holding itself in absolute stillness, looking up at her, as if the thin man had managed to produce a series of perfectly lifelike sculptures to perch atop his hand, each of which he seamlessly replaced with the next.

Anna smiled in spite of herself and reached out her hand to touch the bird. For a moment she thought she might just lay her fingertips on its soft feathers, but in a shocking burst of motion, it flew off, up into the sky, rather than stay and be touched.

The thin man's mouth was locked in an impassive expression, but his sharp eyes flashed with a sort of fire of triumph, and with startling speed and fluency he unfolded himself back to his full height and began to make his way across the road toward Herr Doktor Fuchsmann's shop. Anna was shocked that he could even hear her when she breathed her little question to herself out into the air.

"What was that?" she said.

"That," said the thin man, not turning back, "was a swallow."

The bell on the pharmacy door jingled shut.

It was clear to see, when the thin man pushed his way out of Herr Doktor Fuchsmann's shop, that he had no intention of engaging in further conversation with Anna. His eyes, purpose-made tools for the capture of others like them, swept fluidly past her where she huddled against the wall, without even pausing, and before Anna could push herself to her feet, his gunshot footsteps had carried him halfway to the mouth of the small street.

But Anna had been ready when he came out of the pharmacy.

In a rapid riot of conflicting languages, she answered all his questions.

In Yiddish she said, "I am better now," and then in Russian, "I do not think my father will come back." In German she said, "I am myself," and then in Polish, "And now I am waiting for you."

The tall man was silent for a moment in the street. Any other man alive would've been dumbfounded, but he registered no particular impression at all, only watched Anna closely with dark, evaluative eyes.

When she couldn't wait any longer, Anna added, in French, because it was the closest thing she could think of, "And I don't speak Bird."

This was the first of three times that Anna heard the Swallow Man laugh.

"I don't speak French," he said.

He stood a moment in silence then, watching Anna's stillness, as if waiting to see some sign or signal of what was to come in the expansion and contraction of her small rib cage.

Anna felt herself drowning in the empty stillness. It was the first time she had said it, the very first time she had even allowed herself to think it so clearly:

She did not think her father would come back.

It felt rough and wrong to have said it, like tearing jagged, rusted metal with her bare hands—as if her father had called out to her from across a crowded courtyard and she had heard him and turned away.

Everything was still.

Abruptly the thin man made some sort of decision, and when Anna saw him begin to stride across the way toward her, she was surprised to find herself suddenly frightened.

There was no question that the tall stranger was not a reassuring presence. There was a menace to him, a quiet intensity that was in no way akin to the sort of quality that people cultivate in order to attract the affections of children. All the same, though, there was something in him—perhaps the part that had spoken so easily to the swallow—that fascinated her. He was strange, to be sure, this man, but his was a pungent, familiar sort of strangeness. Perhaps Anna and her father had not had a language of their own—or perhaps their language had been every language. Anna felt irresistibly that in this tall stranger she had found another of their rare tribe—a man of many tongues.

By the time the thin man had, in a few long strides, covered the distance across the road to her, Anna was ready, despite all her fear, to hear that this stranger had been sent to collect her. She was ready to be told that if only she would trust and follow close behind him, she would be taken back to where her father was, that this man had been sent to be her guardian and care-taker until she could be returned to her proper place.

She had decided.

But the man made no such declaration. Instead, crouching down low, he handed her a cookie, exactly like the ones Herr Doktor Fuchsmann had always given her.

Just a cookie.

But in Anna's made-up mind, this was a sort of transub-stantiative miracle; it indicated a kind of transfer of fatherly ordination between Herr Doktor Fuchsmann and the tall man, and this development was better than any of the other pos-sible, more verbal scenarios she could have imagined. Not only was it delicious—this was a kind of magic. And also, it was delicious.

The tall stranger watched with real pleasure as Anna bit into the cookie. She had not eaten in a very long time for a little girl, and certainly nothing so delicious as a buttery, sugary sweet. It wasn't long before the whole thing was gone.

By the time Anna lifted her attention from the suddenly, inconceivably vanished cookie, the thin man had straightened back up and was standing far above her.

"Stay out of sight," he said after a long moment. Turning his eyes back out to Kraków, he added, "For as long as you can."

And then, wooden heel blocks loudly announcing his progress, he walked away from Anna and disappeared into the busyness of the far street.

It was perhaps a bit late, but at age seven Anna was still very much in the process of figuring out how the world really worked. Seven short years had been punctuated by a series of incredible upheavals and overturns in the way that her life functioned—her mother gone, and then a world at war, and now a father disappeared as well. For all she understood, this was The Way of Things. What one knew did not linger; what one expected disappeared. For a coddled girl of seven, then, Anna had become exceedingly skilled at adaptation. Whatever language someone spoke to her was the language she spoke back.

So when the thin man came, speaking to swallows and pulling her favorite cookies out of the air, why should she not have learned to speak his language? And the thin man's language was an erratic, shimmering thing: to soldiers he spoke with an authority that bordered on disdain; to small birds of the air he spoke with gentle tenderness.

And yet there had been something behind his impassive

face as he watched her reach out for the swallow, or taste the sweet stuff of the cookie—there was something in him other than all that dazzle and shimmer, something solid and firm and true. Something hidden.

This was a man who did not always say what he meant or felt.

Anna knew that different languages dealt in nuances of expression with different levels of explicitness—in one tongue an idiom might lay out quite directly what the speaker meant to communicate, whereas in another, via the legerdemain of a self-effacing metaphor, a depth of feeling or a sly opinion might very well only be hinted at.

All this is to say that Anna knew with a startling fury, great enough to give her the strength to tear through cold iron with her own bare hands, that there were other words between those that the tall stranger had said to her.

"Stay out of sight," the tall man had said. "For as long as you can."

Anna smiled to herself. "Here I come."

She had decided.

# Follow the Leader

Anna had never been outside of Kraków, but she had accompanied her father to many of the public gardens of the city before the pall of war had descended, and when, far off ahead of her, she saw the tall stranger reach the hills, she thought with a thrill that he was taking her into the grandest park she had ever seen.

It had not been difficult for Anna to track the thin man through the streets in the city center. He stood at least a head above most everyone he passed, and even from far behind she had no trouble locating the head that sprouted up beyond all the others, so long as she did not allow it to escape around a corner.

What was difficult was staying out of sight, as the thin man had instructed. There are two kinds of children in wartime streets—those who provoke passing adults to turn their heads toward their plight, and those who provoke them to turn away. Anna was, if inconveniently under the present circumstances, fortunate enough to be one of the former; those children who fall into the latter camp are, more often than not, far beyond help.

Nonetheless, Anna very much wanted to avoid attention, and it was not long before she discovered the trick of doing so. A well-fed little girl in a pretty red-and-white dress immediately raises alarm if her face is covered with concern and effort, if she strains to see what is far ahead of her, if she moves only in fits and starts—and this was precisely what her present labor required her to do. At one intersection, though, she felt certain she had seen Monsieur Bouchard, her father's old French friend, in the street ahead, and suddenly, impulsively, abandoning all effort of following the tall stranger, she smiled and ran gleefully toward the familiar man.

In the end he was not Monsieur Bouchard, but the effect of this burst of glee was immediately apparent to her. When she passed through the street hesitantly and with concern, the grown-ups who saw her seemed to latch on to her distress, trying to carry it off with them despite themselves, and the strain of the effort would cause a kind of unwilling connection between the adult and the child until they were out of one another's sight. For the most part Anna felt certain that their intentions were good, but it seemed only a matter of time before someone stopped her, and then she did not know what might happen.

On the other hand, when she ran through the street with a smile of anticipation, passing adults still took notice, but they did not try to carry off her joy with them—instead, it engendered a kindred kind of joy inside of them, and well satisfied with this feeling, particularly in the eternally threatening environment of a military occupation, they continued on their way without giving her a moment's thought.

It was with joy, then, and not concern, that she followed the thin man past the guards at the outskirts of the city—they didn't give her a second glance—and by the time Anna was alone in the twilit hills, this effort of counterfeiting happiness had brought to bear a true sort of excitement within her.

The problem was that the thin man's legs were very long, and every quick stride of his required three or four of her own to match its progress. Now that they were out of the city and out of the sight of its thousand shifting denizens, Anna thought it time for the two of them to reunite; after all, she had fulfilled the task the tall man had set for her, avoiding attention until there seemed to be none left, and now she very much wanted the security of company in the growing dark.

The sun had been gone beyond the horizon for many minutes when the thin man stopped short in the middle of the packed earth path he had been following. His stillness was so sharp and abrupt that Anna herself instinctively froze for a moment before realizing that this was her chance to make up ground.

It was in that moment of stillness that she realized just how cold it had become. The wind whipped around her as she made her way down the hill toward the tall man, but just when she thought she was drawing near enough to call out to him, he turned and, with redoubled speed, lit out into the dark, open pasture to his right.

Without thought Anna followed him.

It was only when she looked over her shoulder, back toward the road, that she saw the bobbing, jostling motion of the beams of flashlights, and heard the clamoring conversation between whoever it was that had been coming down the road.

"Stay out of sight," he had said.

It had been difficult for Anna to keep pace with the thin man before. Now it seemed nearly impossible. He was making his way into the wide fields off the road as quickly and quietly as he could, and as the darkness gathered in around him, Anna began to worry that she would lose sight of him. She broke into a trot, and then into a run, and it seemed to her ages and ages that she ran into the uncharted darkness after the thin stranger.

Before she knew it, the darkness was deep and thick, and she could scarcely see who or what was moving down in the fields ahead of her. She wanted to call out, felt the growing throb of panic in the idea that she might have found a way to make herself yet more alone than she had been before, but something in the notion of raising her voice felt forbidden by the very air that surrounded this tall man. His entire existence was like a giant, silent forefinger raised to the lips of the universe.

*Hush.*

But then she saw it—approaching the thin man in the dark, cutting in quickly from some deeper corner of the pasture, in front of her but behind him—the soft, reflected flicker of a shielded lantern. The flattened glow of the flame was vague, but in the field of sudden night, it shone forth to her eye like a beacon, and she clearly saw the figure of a broad, tight man following after the taut leash of a great dog.

Anna was a young girl of uncommon attention, but it had taken no particular skill to learn, in the Kraków from which she had lately come, what a dog at the end of a taut lead meant.

There was no hesitation in Anna's voice. "Hey!" she called, and again, "Hey!"

Three heads turned swiftly to face her. The tall stranger's response was fluid, nearly seamless, as if Anna and he had rehearsed it.

"Oh!" said the thin man on a breath of unspeakable relief, and dropping the bag that he carried, he ran as quickly as he could to where Anna was standing.

"Thank God," he said. "Are you all right?"

Anna was going to speak, but the thin man smoothed past any moment in which she might've, a swift torrent of chastisement and relieved affection pouring forth from him in "What were you thinkings" and "You had me so worrieds."

With one long hand he gathered Anna in close to his side. With the other he swiftly, deftly pulled the spectacles from his face, depositing them in an inner pocket of his coat, which he closed up to the neck in order to hide the well-tailored suit beneath its wide, upturned lapels.

The broad man and his dog stood where the thin man had dropped his bag, and Anna was now shepherded gently back toward them. She was overwhelmed in the torrent of attention, so much so that when the thin man asked her a direct question, she didn't think to respond.

He stopped and asked again.

"Sweetie—I said, do you promise to be more careful?"

Anna frowned. She had been very careful. It had been the thin man who had not seen the approach of the dog and lantern man. But then again, he had told her to stay out of sight, and she'd very deliberately called attention to herself. Perhaps this was what he meant. She hated breaking the rules and doing the wrong thing, and even this peculiar kind of transgression, of which she had little understanding, engendered real contrition in her.

Anna nodded ruefully. "Yes," she said. "I promise."

The thin man sighed heavily and turned a conspiratorial gaze to the man behind the lantern, as if to say, *Why do children never learn?*

"This must be your land, hm? I'm sorry to have disturbed you. Sweetie, apologize to the man."

By now Anna had admitted her wrongdoing, and in this state no child will fail to apologize, at the very least half-heartedly.

"I'm sorry," she said.

"Thank you," said the thin man. "Ah! We're much later than we said. Grandma will be worried. You have to be more careful!"

Anna couldn't for the life of her think of whom the thin man might be talking about. None of her grandparents were even still alive.

There was no time for questions, though. With fluent but unhurried speech, the thin man turned again to the man behind the lantern and spoke.

"I'm sorry," he said. "I'm all turned around. Can you point me back to the road?"

There was sudden silence.

This was the first moment in which the man of the dog and lantern had been required, even allowed, to speak.

The thin man's question hung in the air.

Anna did not breathe.

Finally the broad man lifted his arm and gestured with the lantern. "That way," he said in rough, rolling Polish. "Ten minutes' walk."

The thin man smiled. "Thank you," he said, and gathering Anna in close, he turned and, with deliberate steps, led her toward the road.

Anna did not know what she'd expected, but it had not been this. They walked silently, the two of them, and the air between them was heavy and hard. Had she been wrong to alert the thin man of the coming danger? Should she have stayed farther out of sight? For the first time since he had handed her the cookie in Kraków, she found herself wondering if, in fact, the tall man had meant for her to follow him in the first place.

But all the same, she had felt real shelter when he had gathered her into his side, felt real concern when he'd run across the field to her. The feeling that she recognized now in the air—this was not a simple, monolithic sense of adult displeasure.

This was a fraught thing—divided, thick with cross-woven and conflicting kinds of worry. Something was going on, something inside the tall stranger, hidden just behind the curtain.

This, Anna knew with perfect, intuitive certainty. She was a child.

At home in Kraków, Anna had developed a habit of understanding people by comparing them to those with whom she was already acquainted—as if she were translating the unfamiliar phrase of each new human being using her full, multilingual range of vocabulary. Frequently when, in the presence of her father, she had been introduced to new people, she had found herself looking forward to a private moment in which she might tell him of whom else this new person was composed:

"Like Mrs. Niemczyk if she had never gotten old, and was not mean."

Or:

"Like Professor Dubrovich if he spoke Madame Barsamian's Polish and had the goofiness of Monsieur Bouchard."

Sometimes, in the course of these descriptions, Anna had hit upon some distinct quality or attribute—the aforementioned goofiness had been one—that was shared amongst many people, and her father had named it for her.

Goofiness.

Resilience.

Assurance.

Deference.

Pride.

Now, trying to understand the thin man, Anna thought that perhaps she had discovered a new example of such a quality.

Of course, the thin man was like her father in his facility with language. That was obvious. But that was not what Anna meant when she thought of daddiness.

Any child who plays out and about in the world quickly learns to distinguish between the grown-ups who have learned to deal with children and those who can be exploited for their lack of such experience—some adult authority is a well-supported fortification, and some is a flimsy, often over-elaborate, unbacked facade. It is a child's business to test these edifices, and Anna had learned as well as any to recognize both kinds.

This quality of daddiness was in part composed, in Anna's mind, of the more experienced sense of authority—but only in part. There was something else, too, something that she struggled to describe to herself, something that made her feel the kind of thorough safety and security that frequently, at the end of a childhood, ceases ever to have existed. This thing was the better half of daddiness. Not every man is in possession of much talent in this area, just as many men cannot sing in tune or compellingly depict a sunset.

But the thin man had many talents.

Not a word had yet been spoken when they reached the road. The thin man had not looked down at Anna once as they walked, but this did not mean that he wasn't watching her.

Anna was well prepared to start back along the dirt track once they found it, but this was not the thin man's intention, and without a word of explanation, he continued on past the path, bending his course to head for a thick stand of trees on the horizon. She was about to ask him where they were going when he broke the silence.

"Thank you," he said. "For warning me."

Anna was terribly confused by this. Was he grateful for what she had done, or angry? She didn't understand. She did, however, know that it was impolite not to answer when someone said thank you.

"You're welcome," she said with as much assurance as she could muster.

The thin man sighed and said, "You did well."

He had slowed his gait significantly out of deference to the difference in their strides, but Anna still had to take two steps to every one of his, and now the only sound that broke the silence of the night was the rapid subdivision in the grass of his footfalls by hers.

Eventually he spoke again. "Listen very closely," he said, slowly releasing another sigh. "The world as it exists is a very, very dangerous place." His voice had turned cold and measured.

Anna was unprepared for the sudden fright and sadness that this statement brought about in her. Usually when adults spoke of danger in her presence, they were quick to assure her that everything would be all right, that she would be safe. The thin man did none of this, and his omission rang out as true in the night as his words had.

Everything he said, even—perhaps especially—the things he left out, seemed to carry the reliable weight of truth.

Anna did her best to choke down her sudden snuffle, but the thin man was perceptive. "Does that frighten you?" he said.

She nodded. "Yes."

The thin man frowned. "Good."

Ahead of them the dark trees loomed up like a clutch of wooden giants, each one an echo of Anna's companion.

"You know people in Kraków?" said the thin man.

Anna nodded.

"People who will take care of you?"

Anna had no good answer for this. Before, she might've said yes, but before, she would've spoken of Herr Doktor Fuchsmann as amongst the very first rank of those who looked after her. What was more, though she never would've allowed herself to admit it, Kraków itself had become threatening. What was that place now, what were its rooms and sidewalks, what was each inch of negative space between the buildings and automobiles and boot heels of the city, if it was not the great open mouth that had swallowed her father up?

For the first time since they'd begun walking together, the tall man looked down at Anna in her silence.

His tone was gently instructive now, and his voice fell into the authoritative lilt of someone well used to imparting information to the less informed. "Listen to me: if you ever doubt that you have something good or comforting to rely upon, then you must assume that you don't." Again the thin man fell silent for a moment. "This is no time for hoping."

Anna didn't answer. Together the two of them crossed in beneath the low hem of the tree branches.

For a longer time again now, they didn't speak. The thin man walked them around and around the thicket of trees, until finally he settled down in a corner far removed from the road. Anna sat down beside him. The ground was cold and hard, and the roots of the trees poked at her uncomfortably.

As soon as she'd squirmed herself into a position she could hold for several minutes at a stretch, the tall man stood up and began to peel layers off of himself. He handed to Anna his long-armed suit coat, which she wrapped around herself gratefully against the cold, and then he shrugged back into his great over-coat.

"In the morning," he said, "I will take you back to Kraków, and we shall find someone to look after you. It is not good for a girl to be without a father these days."

With that, the thin man turned over and closed his eyes.


Anna's heart sank like a heavy stone down into the pool of her gut.

"In the morning," he'd said, "I will take you back to Kraków."

This was impossible. She knew very well that there was no Kraków anymore, at least not in the true sense. She could not be there.

But everything he said was heavy, like truth.

All the same, something bothered Anna about the summary decision that the thin man had made.

She just didn't believe it.

She couldn't stop thinking of the way he had laughed

when she'd spoken to him in all her languages, couldn't stop remembering the glint he'd hidden in the depths of his eyes as he'd watched her reach out for the swallow he had conjured.

To be sure, there were people in the world who seemed to have no use for children, people who had been born with an allergy to anything that stood below hip height—usually people who spent a very long time each day on the appointment of their clothing or facial hair. But was this thin man one of them? Most emphatically not. He was frightening in some ways, certainly—in many ways, even—but he was also bright and exciting and potent.

And good.

Despite the weight of truth in each of his words, to Anna it felt very much like a lie that this man would throw her back unattended into the maelstrom of Kraków.

Anna had always been what adults called "precocious," and this was a word, her father had once upon a time explained, with various uses. To some adults it allowed an escape from the wise clear-sightedness of a child:

"Ah," they would say in the face of an observation of unwelcome young wisdom, "how precocious she is!" and they would move on.

To others it functioned as a reminder of their easy badge of adult supremacy:

"Ah," they would say in the face of some inconveniently valid challenge to their grown-up certitude, "how precocious she is!" and they would move on.

Anna was afraid to ask the thin man the question that

would not leave her mind now—it had the undeniable ring of the questions most often labeled precocious and packed away by adults for later, surreptitious disposal—but she very much wanted to hear, in the truth-laden voice of this tall man, if her father had taught her correctly.

Whenever she had grown indignant at the dismissal of her thoughts and ideas and questions by those adults who had grown too old to see past her precocity, her father had reassured her softly, wiggling his mustache and smiling.

"It's their failure, my little Anna, not yours. Men who try to understand the world without the help of children are like men who try to bake bread without the help of yeast."

This had seemed so true.

She struggled there, beneath the trees, deciding first to speak her precocious question and then to stay silent, over and over and over again, until finally, her mind already half immersed in sleep, she gathered her courage.

"I'm sorry," she said through a wide yawn. "I know it's not good for a girl to be without a father these days. But is it any better for a father to be without a daughter?"

There was silence in the grove of trees for a long moment.

And then she heard the thin man begin to chuckle, low and bright and impossibly sunny in the dark night.

This was the second time that Anna heard the Swallow Man laugh.

\* \* \*

There are those people in the world for whom sleep is an indulgence, and there are those for whom it is a compromise, and Anna had always been one of this second set. In the best of circumstances, she slept lightly and woke early. In the November cold, resting out of doors for the very first time, and beset on all sides with what seemed like the world congress of inconvenient tree roots, she hardly slept at all.

But to say that she hadn't slept only because of the external conditions in which she found herself—this would not have been true.

It was very difficult for her to take her attention away from the thin man, even for a moment. Somewhere, tickling the back of her brain, she felt a certainty that if she wasn't constantly watching this fellow, she would miss whole miracles, whole wonders—things that he let fall incidentally off himself as other men might shed dandruff.

By the time the morning arrived, Anna had made a careful study of the sleeping thin man—his aquiline nose, his broad forehead, the threads of gray in the mad, unraveled tapestry of his hair. He slept with his arms folded, and the long-fingered hand closest to her had wrapped itself almost all the way around his biceps.

There was something in him that needed explanation.

Anna did her best not to think of the drawing of the Alder King at the back of her thick book of stories.

There seemed to be no one moment in which the thin man passed the transition of waking. First he was asleep, his eyes shut, and the very next moment, in precisely the same position, his eyes were open and he was completely alert.

It was with some disappointment that Anna put the thin man's suit coat back into his waiting hand. Even now that the sun was up, the air remained cold, and she would very much have liked some extra warmth to wear.

As he had the night before, the thin man took off his overcoat, but instead of putting his suit jacket back on, he undid the clasp on the top of his physician's bag, and turning to face away from her, he began to change his clothes.

When he turned back to Anna, he was almost completely unrecognizable. A rough, baggy shirt of no color billowed around his narrow chest, and below it he wore a pair of unremarkable, ill-fitting pants, kept up with a shabby leather belt.

This man was not the powerful sophisticate of the city. This was a humble, simple country peasant. Even his overcoat seemed changed—rougher, harder worn—and had Anna not seen him take it off, set it down, and later lift it again from where it had lain to put it back on, she would've thought it another garment entirely.

"You look like a different person," said Anna.

"Yes," said the thin man. "If ever I look too much like myself, you must tell me."

His suit was rolled and deposited into the vacancy in his bag that the rough clothes had left. All things were straightened and fastened and put in place. The thin man lifted his bag and strode out from under the trees, and Anna followed behind him.

It was only a moment before she realized that they were still heading away from the dirt track—and away from Kraków.

Anna faced a terrible dilemma now. No part of her wanted to return to the city. More even than she had the night before, she wished she could stay with this man. She had seen him sleep. She had heard him laugh. She had even come, somehow, to like him. He had spoken truths to her that no one else had dared. Even if they'd hurt.

"The world as it exists is a very, very dangerous place," he had said, and he had not equivocated.

She did not want to go back to Kraków.

But he had told her the night before that that was his plan. And now he was moving away from it. It was not right to pretend that she did not know.

"Um, excuse me?" she said, and with a shock she realized that she did not know a name by which to call out to him.

He was several strides ahead of her now, and at the sound of her voice, the thin man stopped, but he did not turn back to her.

"Yes?" he said.

"I'm sorry," said Anna. "You said you wanted to go to Kraków."

"Yes?" said the tall man.

Anna sighed. "But this isn't the way to Kraków."

Only now did the tall man turn back. He was not smiling, but something in the air he exhaled gave Anna the feeling that he was, and it made her want to smile as well. "No," he said. "It isn't, is it?"

Just as he had in the street across from Herr Doktor Fuchsmann's, the tall man crouched himself down in order to face
her directly.

"Do you want to go back to Kraków?"

He hadn't even finished pronouncing the name of the city
before Anna was shaking her head. "No."

Now something akin to a grin crept into the tall man's
face; his right eyebrow rose slightly, and the right corner of his
mouth bunched up to itself. The movements were tiny, infini-
tesimal shifts, and yet they alone transformed his hard, long
face into something that shone out brightly to her.

"It's not good for a father to be without a daughter, hm?"

Anna was afraid to breathe now, just as she had been before
in the narrow street, lest the swallow should fly away. The thin
man's eyes flicked swiftly over her face, first once, and then a
second time.

And then, in a rush of loose clothing, he straightened up
and began to walk again. Anna ran to catch him. She wanted
to ask what was going on, what he meant by all this, but before she found the words, he spoke, and whatever mirth she
had seen in his face just a moment before was gone from his
voice.

"You must make me two promises," he said.

"OK," said Anna.

"First," said the tall man, "you must always do as you did in
the pasture last night. Do you promise?"

Anna did not know what this meant, but she felt so near to

escaping the empty void of Kraków that she would've promised whatever the thin man had asked of her. "Yes," she said.

"Good," said the tall man. "The second promise you must make to me is that you will ask me every single question that you wish to ask, with no exceptions. But never until we two are alone. Do you promise?"

Anna's brows knit together. "Well," she said. "Yes. I do—but then I have a question."

The thin man turned his head. "Yes?"

"What did you mean, 'Always do as you did in the pasture last night'?"

The thin man frowned and then he said, "The Wisła River passes through Kraków, does it not? You know about rivers?"

Anna nodded.

"A river goes wherever the riverbank does. It never has to ask which way, but only flows along. Yes?"

Anna nodded again.

"Just so," said the thin man. "What I mean, then, is I'll be the riverbank and you be the river. In all things. Can you promise me that?"

Anna nodded a third time. "Yes," she said.

"Very well," said the tall man. "Then you will come with me."

Anna's heart flooded with happiness.

"And someday," said the tall man, "when you are much, much older, you must ask me what erosion is."

\* \* \*

There is a kind of uncontainable, fascinated pride to be had in recovering a thing you think you have lost forever, and every so often that first morning, Anna looked up toward the tall man's sharp-edged face and smiled to herself.

Who was this tall miracle?

Despite what she had feared, he was not like the wicked Alder King. Not really. Anna had never read the story all the way through, but she had opened to its first page in the big book innumerable times, and there, beneath the title of the story, had been an illustration of him, tall and dark and thin, pointing his long finger out across the endless world of the page. She had loved to see that drawing. Looking at the king, narrow and still in his dark black ink, had given her a delicious, secure little fright.

The thin man made her feel the same way, as if whatever danger there was in him—more than a little—somehow belonged to her. As if it was, in some small part, of her doing.

No, the thin man was not like the Alder King, though he didn't lack for similarity. But it would've been a mistake to understand him solely in that way. He was far too good, and he smiled and laughed and he summoned swallows.

In fact, there was another character in Anna's big book of stories that the tall man made her think of just as much as the Alder King. They didn't look nearly as alike, but the second man had been a king as well, very long ago, and he had been a good and wise man. There was a measure of fright to be found in this king, too. He had wanted to cut a baby in half, but it had only been a trick—and a very precocious one, too, Anna had thought—to help return the child to his mother. He had been smart and clever, and what was better, the big book of stories had told her that God had granted him the miraculous ability to speak with birds.

His name was King Solomon.

"Ah!" said Anna with joy in the bright sunlight of midday. "You're Solomon!"

The tall man stopped. "What did you say?"

He did not seem pleased, and suddenly he was far more Alder King than King Solomon.

"You're Solomon," said Anna again.

He shook his head. "No," he said. "I am not. That name isn't safe. No name is."

This introduced a nagging, itchy fear to the back of Anna's head. She had a name. In fact, she had many.

"Names are ways for people to find us," said the tall man. "If you keep a name, people know whom to ask after. And if people know whom to ask after, they can find out where you've been, and that brings them one step closer to finding you. We don't want to be found."

"We don't?"

The thin man shook his head. "No."

This was puzzling. In a very deep place, a room hidden far within her, Anna held, side by side, two twin certainties: that she very much wanted her father to come and find her, and that he would not. "Why don't we want to be found?"

The tall man sighed. "Was your father a nice man?"

"He's the nicest man."

"Do you think he would've left you all alone on purpose?"

"No." But, thought Anna, he *hadn't* left her all alone. He'd left her with Herr Doktor Fuchsmann, and *he'd* left her all alone.

"And don't you think he would've come back to get you if he could've?"

"Of course."

"Well," said the thin man. "Would you like to know why he didn't?"

This was not an easy question to answer, but after some hesitation Anna nodded. She wanted to know most things, if she could stand to.

"Your father did not come back to get you," said the tall man, "because someone found him."

He turned again and began to walk.

Anna felt a deep, sick, plunging sensation somewhere at the very insidest portion of her, somewhere at the very heart of her gut. Just like that, there was no hidden room left inside of her, no space for her secret certainties—there wasn't even an empty void where it had once been. It was just gone. And all her certainties with it.

Her father had been found.

This was the first lesson of the Swallow Man:

*To be found is to be gone forever.*

They walked in the silence for long minutes before Anna spoke.

"But . . . ," she said. "But what happens when I have to call to you?" she said. "What name"—quickly she corrected herself—"what word should I use?"

The tall man thought for a moment without breaking the rhythm of his stride.

"I'll call you Sweetie," he said. "And you call me Daddy."

Anna had no objection to being called Sweetie. "But you're not my daddy."

"No," said the tall man. "But isn't the riverbank the father of the river?"

In silence Anna considered this notion, and above and beside her the thin man thought on a problem of his own.

Abruptly the tall man stopped walking and turned. Only the most important things seemed to make him stop walking, and this would soon become another lesson:

*One can't be found as long as one keeps moving.*

"Listen to me," said the tall man. "I would like to ask you a favor."

Anna nodded.

"Will you give me your name?"

"Anna."

"No," he said, crouching down low. "Give it up to me."

This was confounding and a little bit concerning. Even if she wanted to give up her name, Anna did not at all know how it could be done. "I don't understand. How?"

"Well," said the tall man, "what if we decided that your shoes were mine? I'd still let you use them and walk in them, but they'd belong to me."

"All right," said Anna.

"Your name is just like your shoes," said the tall man. "You don't have to be able to get rid of a thing to give it over to someone else."

"All right," said Anna.

"So," said the thin man. "You'll give your name to me? You still get to hold it, but when someone calls it out, or asks you what yours is, you must remember: "Anna" isn't your name."

The thin man spoke so smoothly and so beautifully, like moving water with a glassy surface, and Anna wanted very much to agree with whatever words floated down on his breath to her. But her name was her very own—perhaps the only thing she really had—and the idea of just giving it away made her chest feel tight.

"But that's not fair," she said.

"Why not?"

"It's *mine*. I *like* it."

The tall man frowned and nodded. "What if I give you something in return?"

"Like what?"

"Well, what seems fair to you?"

Anna did not know what the price of a name should be. All she knew was that she didn't want to give hers up. She liked "Anna," and she liked the people who had used it to call to her. Besides, there wasn't any name, nothing that the tall man liked to be called, that she could take away from him. He *had* no name.

"What name can I take away from you?" she said.

The thin man smiled a thin smile that did not reassure her. "You can't take the name from a nameless man."

This seemed very much to Anna like something the Alder King might say. She suddenly wished he hadn't been so angry when she'd called him Solomon. She wanted him to be like Solomon.

"Let me call you Solomon, and I'll give you my name."

The thin man shook his head without hesitation. "I can't have a name. Particularly not that one."

Anna was not a temperamental child, but this seemed like injustice. She opened her mouth to protest, but with a twinkle in his sharp eye, the thin man stopped her.

"But," he said, "what about something very similar? What about . . ." And here he chirruped and twittered through his lips. "What about 'Swallow Man'?"

Anna couldn't help smiling. "Yeah," she said.

"But only when we're alone. And when we're alone, I'll let you borrow 'Anna' back."

"OK."

"Good. Now, Anna and her daddy and her home in Kraków and everything? That's not yours anymore."

This was very sad.

"It's all right," said the tall man. "I promise I'll keep her safe for you, and you'll have her in the dark, when we're alone."

This made Anna want to cry. What was the use of a name in the dark? But there was not much that the Swallow Man failed to see, particularly things so close to himself. "Someday you can buy your name back from me. I promise."

Anna was dangerously close to asking when, but the Swallow Man quickly turned to walk and continued, "But now that you have no name, you can use any name you like. Even more than one."

This made perfect sense to Anna, and the more she thought of it, the more her understanding unfolded. A name was like a language. If she didn't have one of her own—if "Anna" was not tied to her—she could use whichever one she wanted. She could be whatever she wanted to be.

"And you're the daddy of all my new names, aren't you?"

The Swallow Man smiled. "Yes. I am."

He held out his hand, as a man might do to put the period on a well-struck bargain.

But Anna was not a man, and so she did what any little girl will do when her daddy extends his hand.

She held it.

# A Lesson in Zoology

In 1939 the Germans pushed in from the west, and the Soviets closed in on the east, and between them they split the carcass of Poland. Around, toward, behind, and between these two imperial beasts, Anna and the Swallow Man made it their labor to walk.

The first order of business was to procure for Anna a suit of country clothes. The pretty red-and-white dress in which she had walked out of Kraków was a decent analogue for the Swallow Man's three-piece suit when it came to city clothing—nice enough that it might provoke some passive admiration—but in the country this was no advantage.

The Swallow Man's next lesson:

*Wherever people gather, one ought to appear to them as they themselves would wish to appear. In the city this means looking effortlessly prosperous. In the country this means looking as if one is not from the city.*

Clothing aside, this principle made heavy demands on people aiming to make their lives on the move. Prosperity provides not only for the accumulation of a great number of possessions, but also for their discreet housing in lofty, wide apartments above the ground floor. What kind of prosperous city dweller carries much of anything at all on his or her person? And in the country there was no clearer way to indicate you were from somewhere else than to carry heavy bags.

This was the reason for the Swallow Man's physician's bag. It was not so large that it passed into the realm of conspicuousness, but with careful arrangement he could manage to provision himself decently from what he could fit inside. He packed the bag with extreme deliberation, not only to maximize the space within, but also to avoid any external indication that it might be anything approaching full. In this way he avoided the attention of the curious and the unscrupulous alike.

Inside the bag were the following items:

The two sets of their clothing not currently in use; these the Swallow Man rolled together so tightly that his knuckles turned white with the effort, and Anna sometimes wondered how the garments could ever come apart again when they had need of them.

A German and a Polish passport, neither of which carried a photograph at all resembling the Swallow Man; these were packed away neatly in precisely symmetrical positions opposite one another, against the right and left sides of the bag. In their travels in the eastern, Soviet end of Poland, when he would have occasion to lift a Soviet passport from the body of an old, done-up babushka on the side of the road, he would pack it away at the back edge of the bag, so that his things were flanked on every side but the front by stolen identities.

A small, rectangular hand mirror; this was used mostly to assist the Swallow Man in shaving, which he did every several days using his pocketknife, usually before dawn. It never looked pleasant. But it was one of the Swallow Man's many policies never to go into the city with a face freshly shaven, lest his appearance look too effortfully maintained. By the same token, though, he would never allow his stubble to evolve into a beard— beards held far too much political significance in those days.

A small glass jar of mismatched cigarettes; the Swallow Man hated the smell of tobacco, and when not obliged to present a facade for anyone in particular, he would go to great lengths to avoid its smoke. But as the war wore on, cigarettes came to hold increasing value—they could be given as tokens of goodwill, or traded for other necessaries, and if he thought it important enough, their thoughtless consumption could be displayed as a sign of power or affluence. Also in this jar was a small box of matches that the Swallow Man valued more highly even than others valued cigarettes, and when the time came to use one of them up, he would handle it with reverence and care, as if each were a holy relic or a living thing.

A tin drinking cup; there is abundant fresh water in Poland, and a cup to put it in was all Anna and the Swallow Man ever needed to keep from going thirsty.

A small whetstone; this the Swallow Man used to sharpen his pocketknife every evening before he slept. Whether he gave it two ritual, place-holding strokes or a thorough sharpening depended on the level of its use the foregoing day.

A bright copper pocket watch; the first time Anna saw this, she held it eagerly up to her ear. There had been a huge old cabinet clock in the Łania apartment in Kraków, and one of the things she most missed about her home was the sound of its reliable, limping workings, the *tock* just a touch longer than the *tick*. She was, however, disappointed to find that the watch was broken and made no sound of any kind. When, on very rare occasion, Anna and the Swallow Man were obliged to sleep amongst other people, in place of sharpening his knife (which he preferred to keep hidden from others unless its use was unavoidable) the Swallow Man would ineffectually wind the broken copper watch.

And a heavy fountain pen in a small wooden case; the initials *DWR* were painted on the top in faded red. This pen remained in its case, and the case in the bag, almost always.

Outside the bag the Swallow Man carried these items:

The wide black umbrella; it was of great use not only in the rain, but also in the snowy months, which were many. More than once the Swallow Man carved a small notch out of Poland—with his fingers when the earth was soft enough, with his pocketknife when it was not—and stuck the umbrella in to keep the falling snow off while Anna and he slept. They would frequently awaken curled up beneath an umbrella groaning under the weight of the snow, but it never failed to stay up. This umbrella was the Swallow Man's only constant concession to comfort. Every year when the temperature began to grow truly cold, of course, out of necessity they acquired, frequently by easy theft or other unauthorized means, heavy coats, hats, and, if they could be found, suitable gloves (the Swallow Man's narrow hands and long fingers almost never fit into a pair). Even so, when the warmth returned, their precious winter-weather comforts would simply be abandoned in a heap on the ground. They could not be transported easily if they were not worn—coats particularly—and winter wear in the summer months was a clear sign of vagrancy. Whether one truly was vagrant or not, its advertisement was held an untrustworthy quality, and nothing was more anathema to the Swallow Man than untrustworthiness.

His pocketknife.

His round, gold-rimmed spectacles in a soft tan leather case; these the Swallow Man needed very much in order to see at any distance, but he categorically refused to wear them outside of a city setting. "They make me look too intelligent," he said. "One can't go about looking intelligent." Frequently, in the country, he would take them out to survey the land ahead or to examine some far-off, unknowing person, but they would never stay out for long.

A brown glass flask that contained no liquor, but rather a multitude of tiny white pills; in the beginning the Swallow Man tried not to let Anna see these tablets or their consumption, but he took them meticulously, three times a day, and eventually it became untenable to keep the practice hidden. Anna was familiar with pills. In her mind they were harbingers of trouble rather than wardens against it, but she never asked about them. By now she knew the difference between those secrets they shared and those that the Swallow Man held hidden. If he hadn't wanted her to see in the first place, what good could possibly come of asking? In addition, the Swallow Man kept a large bottle of the tablets in his bag as an emergency reserve, the secrecy of which he never relaxed. Twice they had to return to a sizable city in order to find more.

And money, if there was any, which, almost always, there was not; even when there was an opportunity to acquire some, they frequently passed it by. Money has a peculiar effect on otherwise generous and friendly people and has the tendency to make them avaricious. Even the most gentle farmsteader who fully intended to allow this tall stranger to split some paltry, nominal amount of wood in exchange for a couple of small loaves of bread; even the traveling salesman who was going to throw the rest of his cheese to the dogs so as to avoid having to carry it along with him; even the marketer returning home who took pity on the man and his daughter, very much wanting to give them one of the chickens she had failed to sell that day when they parted ways—none of them would have been as friendly if the sight, the smell, even the thought, of money had entered into the deal. Money divides people into buyers and sellers. The Swallow Man wanted to meet a person only if he could make that person a comrade or a friend for the brief duration of their acquaintance, and it is a heavy task for buyers and sellers truly to be friends. The liabilities of money far outweighed its advantages.

And all of these things were carried while carefully maintaining the impression that Anna and the Swallow Man had thoughtlessly stepped out the door no longer than a bare hour or two before.

For the most part, each of these individual objects was a constant companion, but clothing a growing girl is, under the best of circumstances, something of an undertaking, and on the road it was terribly troublesome. Far more often than the Swallow Man would've liked, one dress had to be changed for the next.

The red-and-white dress did fine for city clothing in the beginning—cities were, in the main, avoided anyhow, and it spent most of its time rolled tightly between the vest and jacket of the Swallow Man's suit. And as long as one was not scrupulously honest, it was never such a great feat to find a simple, modest dress for the wilderness with enough room for growing into.

Of course, when the time came to make a visit to a city and the red-and-white dress came out of the physician's bag again, it had grown hopelessly small for Anna, and against the Swallow Man's better judgment, he left her outside of Gdańsk for an hour while he went to procure something new.

The Swallow Man seemed quite ambivalent about Anna's safety, particularly as it related to cities. At first he took very close care of her, making certain, whether on the road or off, in the country or outside a town, to keep her near. But as time wore on and she came to understand the lessons and principles by which they navigated their life, his care began to slacken, and he seemed, for lack of a better phrase, to begin to trust her much more with her own self.

Of course, this did not last. The world was closing around

them like a fist, tighter and tighter with every passing week, and Anna grew older and taller and her body began to change, and the question of whether it was safer to take her into the city or leave her outside of it became more and more difficult to answer simply.

"Why must you grow?" the Swallow Man asked on one occasion. "Really. It's very inconvenient." Anna was not sure whether or not he was joking, but this was an uncertainty she encountered frequently.

Her father, on the other hand, had always been a joker, though a sensible one—he'd smiled wide beneath his mustache or laughed in celebration of his own jokes. The most Anna could hope for from the Swallow Man was some tiny, secreted fragment of a smile.

He never smiled at all, though, when Anna complained that her shoes were becoming too small. Shoes were a particular and grave hardship to the Swallow Man.

The Swallow Man had sturdy boots of wood and leather that kept his feet warm, dry, and strong throughout the year, and when he had to appear in the city, he could easily spend half a day shining them up and no one would be the wiser. His fine heel blocks did begin to wear and round with the constant roughness of the road, but Anna was the only one who seemed to notice that.

She, though, had been wearing a pair of shiny little red shoes the day the Swallow Man led her out of Kraków—the most ill-suited things imaginable for any sort of serious travel—and at that time winter had been fast approaching. The Swallow Man managed to find her a good pair of boots in a village several weeks later, but they were on the small side to begin with, and by the end of the season, they squeezed her feet intolerably. She could barely get them back on when she had necessity to take them off, and no matter how many pairs they went through, this problem almost never seemed to recede.

"Why must you grow?" the Swallow Man had asked.

The grief of little girls' shoes contributed a great number of wrinkles to the Swallow Man's sharp face, as if the look of the battered old leather of each successive pair were contagious and left its lingering mark on him long after the shoes had been cast aside. This, Anna had no trouble seeing.

But Anna saw this grief the way the upward-facing trunk of a tree might see its foliage—she rightly assumed it was an outgrowth of her own self, but she never saw the thick, dense, monolithic root system out of which she herself grew.

This is what Anna did not know:

Another constant companion traveled with them in the company of the knife and the watch and the glasses and the pills. The Swallow Man kept it wrapped up in clean white cotton in a little bundle, safe within the physician's bag: one rigid, beaded handmade baby shoe.

Anna did not know about it, because the Swallow Man almost never took it out once they began to travel together, and when he did, it was only long after she was asleep. Even so, he worried constantly that the tiny beads of pink and white and gold were falling off with each jostling step of his constant motion through the world, though in truth it was usually the unwrapping of the thing to check the damage that pulled them loose.

Of course, what Anna *did* know was not wrong—the very real, very practical, continual problem of her inadequate shoeing caused the Swallow Man very real and very practical grief— but what she did *not* know was no less true: the Swallow Man grieved because he could not think of little girls' shoes without thinking of little girls' shoes.

This was the sum total of all the things that the Swallow Man had elected to carry with him out of desire. There was one other secret thing, though, that Anna and the Swallow Man carried along with them out of necessity:

At the very bottom of the Swallow Man's bag, where hands could be laid upon it only deliberately, was a peculiar seven-shot revolver and a small cardboard box of cartridges.

The Swallow Man was meticulous in the observation of his strategy for living in the odd, angry place that the world became in those years. He had many lessons to teach Anna, and over time his lessons began to describe the outline of the several guiding principles that governed his strategy.

The first and perhaps most significant of these principles was this:

*People are dangerous. And the more people there are in one place, the more dangerous the place becomes.* This was true of buildings, of roads, of towns, and of cities. It was particularly true of the encampments and factories that seemed to be popping up everywhere in the wilderness, and the Swallow Man gave their smoke-stacks a wide berth whenever he saw them on the horizon.

The second principle that guided the Swallow Man was this:
*Human beings are the best hope in the world of other human beings to survive. And as the number of human beings other than oneself in a particular place at a particular time approaches one, the hope of help rises exponentially.*

Of course, the Swallow Man curated the first impressions of these new people carefully. He never spoke to strangers first, preferring to allow them to reveal their language and accent to him, and once they had, it was a rare occasion upon which he didn't closely match them. This went a very far length toward putting them at their ease.

Mostly he was scrupulous. Mostly he did not take what was not given, and when he did, it tended to be from the unfriendly or the hostile. But Anna did learn, in his company, to be wary of the agility of long fingers.

He did not prefer to take, though—he preferred to speak and to listen.

The Swallow Man was a master conversationalist, finding and assuming the role best suited to each new acquaintance's personality, whoever that person might turn out to be. With some he would nod softly without much speaking at all, while with others he would consider quietly what it interested his new acquaintance to say, and at a precisely selected moment, he would ask a simple question that would turn an otherwise taciturn individual into a whirlwind of animated speech. With still others Anna watched him speak at length, telling incredibly textured stories of his past, no two of which were ever the same, or even particularly consistent.

These she liked best.

Sometimes the Swallow Man's discussions would last great swaths of the day, and other times no more than half an hour's time. However long he spent with his strangers, though, Anna found that, more often than not, whatever the Swallow Man had come wanting would be offered to him without his ever asking for it.

Another lesson:

*Asking a stranger for something is the easiest way to ensure that he will not give it. Much better simply to show him a friend with a need.*

At first Anna was not permitted to speak during these encounters. The Swallow Man frequently referred to her obliquely, sometimes even directly asking her questions, but each of these was calculated to appear as if it might have an answer, while Anna herself knew it did not. She knew the rule—he was the riverbank. She would remain silent, and the Swallow Man would shrug and sigh. "She's a little bit shy today."

This suited Anna perfectly—until one day the Swallow Man told a truck driver that her mother had left her with him and run off.

"Poor girl," the truck driver had said, frowning, but Anna was incredulous. Her mother had not abandoned her. She would never have done such a thing, and Anna was shocked that the Swallow Man would have said so.

"No!" said Anna, aggrieved.

In the moment it did not seem to be any huge transgression.

The Swallow Man smiled and shook his head at the truck driver, saying something like, "No, of course not, Sweetie. Daddy was just telling a joke," but as soon as the truck disappeared over the horizon, the Swallow Man turned. His eyes were dark and cold.

"Why did you do that?" He was as hurt as he was angry, but Anna explained that her mother had been lovely and kind and would never have left her, and if his face didn't precisely soften, the little warm light did rekindle itself, far, far behind the Swallow Man's eyes.

"But, Sweetie," said the Swallow Man. "Don't you remember? That's *Anna's* mother you're talking about."

She had forgotten, and the embarrassment of this oversight only swelled her upset. "Well, Sweetie has too many mothers and I don't know any of them and I can't keep them straight, and whenever you say 'Mama,' I think of Anna's mama, and it's *not true, I'm Anna.*"

The Swallow Man sat lightly down on the dusty side of the road opposite her. Even so, she had to crane her neck to look up and see his face.

"Can I tell you something?" he said. His voice was almost always soft, but now it was soft and gentle. "I miss all our friends. I remember every one of them, all those people whom we meet on the road or talk to in front of a cottage hearth. I really do. Sometimes I think about one of them before I fall asleep, or I remember one of them while we're walking, one of them whom I haven't thought about in a very long time, and it makes me sad, wondering if they're still OK. Do you know why?"

Anna frowned. "Why?"

"Because it's real. Everything. Just because I give them names that are not my own and tell them about things that didn't happen, it doesn't mean it's fake. We still become friends. I still care about them."

"But you're *lying*. Lies are *bad*. Everyone says."

The Swallow Man leaned back. "How do you say 'bird' in French?"

*"Oiseau."*

"In German?"

*"Vogel."*

"And in Russian?"

*"Птица."*

"Did you lie about any of those?"

"No! I swear! That's how you say it!"

"I know it is. The thing is, I'm trying to teach you a whole new language. My language: Road. And in Road there's more than one way to say everything. It's very tricky. In Road, if you say, 'My mother left me with Sergei Grigorovich and ran off,' you might very well be saying, 'My mother is gone and now I travel with my Swallow Man.' You might also be saying, 'I don't remember my mother and it makes me sad to think about her.' It's very simple to translate something into Road, but it's very difficult to translate anything back."

Anna wanted this not to make sense. Try as she might, though, she couldn't help but see the logic in it.

"Speaking Road is different from lying?"

"They couldn't *be* more different. In Road there *is* no way to lie."

This also made its own sense. "'Swallow Man' is in Road, isn't it?"

The Swallow Man nodded.

"Is anything else you said to me in Road?"

"No."

The Swallow Man got up and started walking again, and Anna followed after him. The deluge that had overflowed the riverbank swirled quietly in her chest now, captured in a perfectly round little pool of the Swallow Man's making.

She was relatively certain he was telling the truth, but nonetheless, Anna couldn't help wondering what "no" might mean in Road.

Anna was very precocious.


Anna and the Swallow Man never had much trouble with the people they met. Of course, that was due in large part to the fact that they almost only ever met people they wanted to meet—new friends for the Swallow Man's vast catalog. On rare occasion they would, by chance, encounter someone unfriendly, but these people were mostly suspicious, or put upon, and they only wanted to be alone. Once they were surreptitiously unburdened of whatever it was that the Swallow Man had need of, they were easily obliged.

There was, however, another category of person that did not fit into the Swallow Man's system of understanding:

Soldiers were unlikely ever to increase the odds of a person's survival.

As the time went on, Anna began to see more and more soldiers, not just at crossroads and border checkpoints and city gates, but walking through fields or sleeping in forests.

After a certain point it was difficult to find new friends to meet, for all the soldiers between them.

The Swallow Man explained them like this:

"Those look like young men, don't they? But they're not. The ones from the west—those are wolves. And the ones from the east are bears. They disguise themselves as young men because it's easier for them to travel in human places like roads and cities that way. Can you imagine how foolish a wolf would look trying to drive an automobile?

"The Wolves and the Bears, neither of them like human beings at all, and if they can find a reason to hurt you, they will. They're here because they want the world to be full of animals like them. They're making as much space as they can, and they make space by getting rid of people, and at any moment that people could be you.

"Of course, there's a way around this. If you can make one of them wonder if you, like him, are not a person but a disguised Wolf or Bear, he will likely let you pass by in safety. This is a very useful technique, but it is easier accomplished with Bears than with Wolves. I will tell you why.

"Wolves define themselves by what they are. They form a pack, and only other Wolves like them are admitted to it. A Wolf decides who he is by looking around and seeing what kinds there are in his pack. If there are big Wolves in the pack, he says to himself, 'I must be big!' If the pack is made up of purple

Wolves, a Wolf will surely decide, regardless of the color of his own fur, that he, too, is purple. One day, one hopes, the members of the pack may begin seeing good, kind Wolves around them, but for the moment it is a particularly cruel and angry pack that the Wolves inhabit. But that is the Wolf's delusion: he mistakes himself for his friend.

"The Bear's delusion is a bit more peculiar, but once one understands it, it is rather easier to take advantage of. The Bears, unlike the Wolves, do not define themselves by the things that they, taken as a pack, are. The Bears do not think of themselves as a pack. Bears are solitary animals. They think of themselves as one gargantuan Bear that spans half the globe. They understand what that Bear is not by looking at what other Bears *are*, but by looking at what they, the great global Bear, *do*. These days the Bear works hard at its labor and proclaims itself proud to be a Bear. And it is much easier to convince someone that you work and are proud than it is to convince him that you, like him, are cruel and angry."

"Why?"

"Wolves are never cruel and angry toward other Wolves. How should you convince a Wolf that you are a cruel and angry Wolf when you cannot treat him cruelly or angrily, and you do not look like a Wolf?"

This was a good question.

"It would be much easier for you to convince a Bear that you are like him than a Wolf, but in either case you should avoid a soldier at all costs if I am not with you. They are dangerous. They want nothing more than to hurt you."

"How do I know if a soldier is a Bear or a Wolf?"

"Generally, the Bears wear brown coats and the Wolves wear gray."

"Not purple?"

"Not purple. But anyone wearing any red at all ought to be avoided. The dukes and captains of Wolves and Bears frequently wear red somewhere on themselves."

"Oh."

Anna couldn't help remembering that the Swallow Man's tie had been red when first she met him in Kraków. In happy moments when she thought of this, she assumed it must have been because he was a duke of some sort, or maybe a prince. Anna loved hearing the stories he told about himself to the people they met on highways and paths, but she knew they were all in Road, and she wondered about who he was in other languages.

In one particularly upsetting moment, Anna thought of the Swallow Man's red tie and wondered just how cruel and angry a captain of Wolves would have to be in order to lay such a deep trap for a little human girl.

But Anna knew her Swallow Man, and whatever he was, he was not an angry man.

And she had not yet seen him cruel.


Borders were everywhere in those days. The Swallow Man preferred to avoid them as well as could be, but if one walks for long enough, no matter what the direction, eventually a boundary will need crossing over. When they had to do so, it was much preferable to pass by soldiers than to risk being seen sneaking—better, said the Swallow Man, to be where one is meant to be, if you're going to be caught. Better not to risk being seen for what they think you are.

The Swallow Man's strategy for passing through checkpoints was much more regimented than his strategy for finding new friends, and Anna had an indispensable role to play in the performance. In the days leading up to a planned border crossing, the two of them would spend much of their time searching the nearby forests and farms to find something small and sweet for her to carry. An apple was ideal, but could be found only in certain months. Anything sweet and natural, though—a handful of cherries or small wild strawberries—would do.

In winter, when nothing grew, they did their best not to cross through checkpoints at all.

Everything living tightens and contracts in the cold of winter. This includes borders and their small gaps.

If Anna and the Swallow Man were to pass by Wolfish soldiers, they would take their time in careful preparation and don their city clothes. If the soldiers were Ursine, they would remain in their walking outfits, but in either case, as they approached the checkpoint, Anna would lag slightly behind her daddy and eat idly at her sweet thing. She would not speak.

Usually there was a pair of soldiers to pass between, and the first and perhaps most crucial part of the crossing ritual was the Swallow Man's selection of which of the two he would speak with. For this reason he preferred checkpoints that stood at a short distance from tree cover or, perhaps, a bend in the road—too much distance to cross and they would be seen by the soldiers long before he could greet them, and the choice would be lost; too little distance and the Swallow Man's great height might set them on guard.

He never had long to decide which soldier he liked better—only moments, really—and when they were crossing the Bear's border, he would have to do it all without his spectacles. Once he had chosen, he would smile, fix his eyes upon his soldier, and raise his hand in a neutral, friendly wave.

Invariably, the greeting he would receive in return would be curt, in some cases even bored. Never did a soldier return a smile of his own accord. More often than not, the response consisted of a simple *"Papiere, bitte"* or, in the case of a Bear or a particularly invested Wolf, *"Dokumenty,"* the word in both Russian and Polish. This slightly hostile starting point was fine with the Swallow Man—even preferable. People (including wild beasts in disguise) are more confident in their decisions when they think they have changed their own minds.

Generally, this demand—a bare word or two—was all the Swallow Man would have to go on for a regional accent, but he was very skilled, and he would take a moment, muttering to himself, rummaging in his physician's bag.

"Ah!" he would say in the soldier's language and dialect. "Of course. Papers, papers, papers . . ." In truth, he knew precisely where in the bag the proper document could be found, but he never seemed to manage to lay a hand on it until the soldier invariably asked, "You are German?" or "You are Russian?"

It was from these border crossings that Anna's mind

gleaned the certainty that all the world's Bears came from Russia and all the world's Wolves from Germany.

When the question had been asked, the Swallow Man would hold up the appropriate passport and flash a smile of quiet pride. This moment never failed to terrify Anna. It was perhaps the most delicate of the entire interaction, and she knew full well that should the soldier choose to look inside the passbook—the natural enough next step in the process—then he would easily uncover the entire deception.

The timing of the document's transfer from the Swallow Man's hand to the soldier's was crucial. He had to begin asking his question before offering the passport for inspection, so that the soldier would answer before opening it, but he couldn't afford to appear to be dallying.

"Where," the Swallow Man would ask, "are you from?" Each time, the question sounded offhanded, obligatory, almost as if it were a slight imposition to him to have asked it in the first place.

No matter what town or district name passed the lips of the soldier, the Swallow Man's eyes would crack open wide and he would find himself laughing with thorough, genuine, surprised delight. It was a reaction that could come only from a fellow hometowner—the joyful surprise of hearing the name of a cherished place when you stand as far away from it now as you ever have in your life.

At first Anna could not believe how seamlessly his falsehood could counterfeit truth. After all, she saw him react, if not precisely the same way, then certainly with no less delight and surprise at hearing words as far-flung and strange as Lindau,

Zaraysk, Makhachkala, Quedlinburg, Gräfenhainichen, Mglin, and Suhl, words that might as well have stood for stars in the farthest reaches of the sky, for all she knew of them. But she soon came to understand that this was not falsehood at all.

The practice of lying is concerned with attempting to overlay a thin paper substitute atop the world that exists in order that it seem to suit your purposes. But the Swallow Man didn't need the world to suit him. He could make himself suit whatever world it pleased him to agree existed. This was what it was to be a native speaker of Road.

The cornerstone of their success in border crossing was that the Swallow Man never, ever said directly that he was from the places the soldiers named. People (including wild beasts in disguise) are far more confident in their decisions when they think they have changed their own minds themselves.

Instead of giving a simple lie, the Swallow Man would launch into a series of questions and appreciations.

"Why can't they make beer here like they do at home?" he would say. "What I wouldn't give for a glass of *real* lager." Even if a particular soldier wasn't partial to beer (but what young man isn't?), none would deny that his hometown had the best of anything.

Or perhaps he would say, "How's the old Prospekt Lenina?" There was hardly a single town in all of the Soviet Union without a Lenin Street anymore.

Or: "Oh!" he would cry. "I missed the *Platz* so much this *Weihnacht*. Most beautiful time of year."

What German town didn't have a square? What town

square wasn't amply decorated for Christmas? What young man didn't miss home when the holiday came and he was off tramping around through some godforsaken Polish field?

It would not take the Swallow Man long to get a smile or an agreement out of the soldier, and when Anna saw this, it was her time to speak up.

"Daddy?" she would say, and the first time the Swallow Man would dismiss her.

"One moment, Sweetie."

Anna would wait a moment then, giving him just enough time to pull the soldier back into discussion, but not so much that he could be caught out on any particular specific detail. Again she would say, "Daddy?" and this time the Swallow Man would turn and crouch down next to her, and flashing an apologetic smile to the soldiers, he would say, "What is it, Sweetie?" and she would ask him her question.

"Do soldiers like strawberries, too?"

They'd hit upon this question by accident. At first the plan had simply been for Anna to hold up the fruit to the soldier wordlessly, but when first they'd crossed a border, Anna had become frightened at the last moment, unsure of whether Wolves and Bears and other wild beasts even ate fruit.

So she'd asked, and the effect had been magical.

The Swallow Man would answer, "Oh, Sweetie, I think they'd like them very much."

When she first began to travel with the Swallow Man, Anna looked even younger than she was, and the Swallow Man showed her how to wipe the loose hair out of her face with the flat palm of her hand, like younger girls still did. She would hold up her sweet thing to the second soldier first—the silent man to whom her daddy had not spoken—and then the other, and their mouths full of sweetness, they never seemed to remember to look at the passport before handing it back to the Swallow Man.

In this way Anna and the Swallow Man tamed wild beasts with wild fruit.


Most of the time Anna spent with the Swallow Man, though, was spent not meeting strangers or passing border guards, but walking through Poland.

Poland is, despite (or perhaps, in part, because of) all her bloodshed, a country of singular magic. Everything in the world exists in Poland, and exists in an old and silent way that is somehow more than natural. Anna took great delight in all the new things that there were to see and learn about, and the Swallow Man was an excellent teacher. Before very long she could recite the scientific names of the vast majority of the different varieties of trees and plants that watched them pass by, and she had soon chosen her favorites from their overgrown ranks.

It was only thanks to the Swallow Man's encyclopedic knowledge that they didn't starve in the wild. Of course, it took time to adapt. Anna always preferred when there was someone carrying bread or meat to befriend, but when there was not, the Swallow Man knew well which roots were good to eat, which berries were safe, which fruits yielded a good nut or seed, and which leaves left a sweet taste in the mouth and which a bitter, and over time it became no longer a strange thing to go a week or maybe two eating nothing but Poland.

The forests seemed to bring out the instructor in him, and in those places where growing, living things thrived, the Swallow Man talked the most.

Sometimes in the hills and plains, though, they would go an entire day or two together without speaking, walking in parallel at a distance of fifty or a hundred yards through dewy, tall green grasses. The Swallow Man never told Anna to stay close, never chided her for wandering, and in angry or tired or hungry moments, she sometimes wondered if he would even have noticed if she had simply gone off in a different direction and never come back.

Of course, even when she was angry, this bitter speculation couldn't last long. Whenever a plume of smoke rose beyond the horizon, or the noise of an engine or a raised voice reached their ears, the Swallow Man hurried back to Anna's side as swiftly as she hurried to his.

If the forests made him instructive and the hills and plains made him reflective, nothing pleased the Swallow Man better than the wetlands.

There is a great system of lakes and rivers and marshes that occupies more than six hundred miles of Poland's northeast, and they returned to this stretch with disproportionate frequency.

There was, of course, a significant risk to them there—for those who walk, nothing is more important than one's feet, and there is nearly no danger so insidious to feet than the damp that does not dry. For this reason they most often wandered the wooded areas of higher elevation that dotted the marshes. Only in those places did the Swallow Man ever stop to sit simply for the pleasure of it.

There were masses of birds there, birds that the Swallow Man loved to watch in flight. These Anna learned to identify as well, but by their common names, like friends. If the Swallow Man knew their scientific names, he did not use them, and he pointed them out for Anna's admiration and not her study.

There were fish to catch there, and few other people that might catch them. Some of their best days were spent in those wetlands, and it was always a sad occasion when the Swallow Man led Anna away from them.

It was one such day, as their second winter approached, walking up and away from the low wetlands, tired and fearful of the coming cold, that she finally asked the question that had been dogging her mind for months and months.

The Swallow Man walked ahead of her that day. The truth was that she didn't enjoy the wetlands as much as her Swallow Man did—there was something in the smell of the sitting water that she never found entirely palatable—but she was dragging her heels nonetheless, wishing to stay where they were as long as possible, as if their mere presence in the wetlands might ward off the coming cold. At least, this was what she told herself. In truth, her reluctance had much less to do with the cold or the wetlands than it did with the Swallow Man himself.

It was not ever, under normal circumstances, entirely clear to Anna that the Swallow Man was human in the same way that she was. He was systematically aloof, he could operate as if the world were other than it was, and the moments when she most wanted to know what he was thinking were the moments in which it was least likely that she would be able to tell.

But in the wetlands he relaxed. In the wetlands he was closer to being something she knew how to understand, and it was this more than anything that she desired. She had long since abandoned the project of assembling an analogy to describe him out of people she had known before—the fact was that there was simply no one like him—but she still wanted to know who he was beneath all his long fingers and stubble and Road speech. She wanted to know what language his heart spoke.

And so she dragged her heels, and she asked her question to the back of his head.

"Swallow Man?" she said. "Where are we going?"

The Swallow Man stopped and turned. He did not immediately have an answer for her.

This might seem as if it were a pointed question, intended to highlight Anna's weariness—after all, by this point they had been walking over a year, and they showed no sign of stopping—but the truth was, naive as it must seem, that Anna was convinced there was some direction to their wanderings. The Swallow Man always had very particular ideas about where they ought to be heading and always decided their direction with authority. What was more, he seemed completely certain of and invested in his decisions, even when those decisions took them near to cities or across checkpoints.

How could this be explained, if not by some destination or plan?

The question caught the Swallow Man off guard, but perhaps unsurprisingly, it did not take him terribly long to find an answer for Anna.

"Ah!" said the Swallow Man, hatching a secret grin at the corner of his cheek. "I'm glad you asked. I've been wanting to tell you, but I wasn't sure you were old enough to know yet."

"I'm old enough."

"Are you sure?" The Swallow Man raised his eyebrow.

"Of course I am. Tell me!"

"Well," said the Swallow Man. "You and I are on a mission of crucial scientific significance." This he said with such somber intention that the ache in Anna's feet was swept momentarily away in her madness of pride.

"We are?"

"We are. Do you know what an endangered species is?"

"No." At first Anna had been embarrassed by the things that she did not know, but by now she had seen that there was no shame in learning. Besides, no one could possibly know everything the Swallow Man knew.

"A species is a kind of animal," he said. "And to say that a species is endangered means that for one reason or another there are almost none of them left."

"Oh," said Anna. This was sad. "I don't like that."

The Swallow Man shook his head. "Me neither. That's why we're out here. There's a bird in this country, an extremely rare bird that's very, very endangered. There's only one left. And I want to save it. The Wolves and the Bears desperately want to find the bird, because it tastes delicious—and because it's the last, they think that whoever eats it will become very, very strong."

This seemed like a peculiar injustice to Anna, and somehow a terribly personal one. She understood well that Wolves and Bears hated humans, but this seemed like the natural order of things—in every story she knew, beasts were the enemies of people. But to wipe out a kind of thing entirely . . .

"But there's only one of them left!" she said.

"That's right. The Wolves and the Bears have eaten the rest. I'm going to make sure the last one stays safe."

"Wow."

The Swallow Man nodded. "It's not always so easy to find, our bird—it's quite shy. But if you know the signs it leaves behind, it's no great task to track it. This is the one advantage you and I have over the Bears and Wolves: their weapons are their teeth and their claws—"

"And their rifles." Rifles had become a particular fascination of Anna's in her crossing of borders. She did not know for certain what they did, but by now she knew very well that they were dangerous, and that every soldier carried one.

"And their rifles," agreed the Swallow Man. "But our weapons? Our weapons are knowledge and observation and patience and time, and given enough of those last two, *our* weapons will always prevail."

This, of course, was true. Anna didn't know precisely what it meant, but it sounded terribly wise, and so she nodded. "What makes the bird so special?"

The Swallow Man sighed, deep and heavy. For the first time he seemed somehow upset at Anna's question, and she couldn't help wondering if it was because the answer was obvious or because it was obscure.

"What makes it special?" said the Swallow Man. "It's a bird. A bird that flies and sings. And if the Wolves and Bears have their way, no one will ever fly or sing in precisely the same way that it does. Never again. Does it need to be more special than that?"

For this, Anna had no answer, but she could not tell if it was because the answer was obvious or because it was obscure.

"Will you help me keep it alive?"

Nothing could've stopped her. Anna nodded her head furiously. "But how can I? I don't know its signs."

The Swallow Man nodded. "I'll teach you. Someday. For now, the first step is that *you* must stay safe. Stay alive. If there's no one around to keep the *bird* safe, then the Wolves and Bears will get her for sure."

"All right. But you stay safe, too, OK? And alive."

The Swallow Man nodded solemnly. "OK."

He turned back to the road, and after a moment's walk he called back over his shoulder.

"How do your shoes feel?"

# The Man Who kissed His Rifle

Winter was different.

In winter the ground hardens, and the trees are bare and will not hide you, and the earth shows your footprints in the snow wherever you go. Food is scarce, and there is almost no hope of finding enough to fill your belly where there are not people.

Anna and the Swallow Man resisted the beginning of winter as long as they could. As long as they could gain some nutritional benefit from the earth, they kept on the move, taking pains to traverse only the most remote ground on the days when snow had fallen. But there would always come a point when, exhausted and hungry and cold, they would have no choice but to concede that winter had descended on them. Anna reached this point a day or two before the Swallow Man did, and if it was a disappointment that they would not be able to avoid wintering that year, it was also a relief to her when finally they settled in.

In order to successfully survive the winter, they needed to be near people. Despite the Swallow Man's guiding principles, in the case of the winter, it was foolish to look for a small collection; if they'd settled near such a population—a farming village, say—their presence would almost certainly have been quickly found out. Where there are only so many people, there is only so much food, and where there is only so much food, the amount that can disappear without notice can only ever be so large. And they had two bellies to fill.

This did not, however, mean that the Swallow Man's principle was ill founded; it was certainly correct, and the more people there were in a particular place, the greater the chance of accidental discovery, or of some inconvenient insomniac catching sight of a strange little girl with an armful of purloined potatoes—and this in addition to the more general danger of Wolves and Bears and those that served them.

In the winter that straddled the years of 1940 and 1941, their second winter together, Anna and the Swallow Man found an almost optimal situation: a town of middling size with only a nominal Wolfish presence, and nearly an hour's journey away, mostly through forest, a set of boulders resting in just such a way as to shelter a small triangle of earth between them almost entirely from the wind and snow. It was in this place, no larger than a particularly self-afflicting monk's cell, that Anna and the Swallow Man spent the winter.

It is only once one stops that one realizes just how much time and attention walking really consumes. Sitting close to one another in a small enclosure of stone for the length of a season, Anna and the Swallow Man did the only natural thing there was to do to pass the time: they told stories. Or more specifically, the Swallow Man told stories.

They were good stories, captivating and compelling, and Anna listened with every tiny bit of her being, listened with a fury to close out the cold: stories of men who battled Wolves and Bears and Jackals and Tigers (who were like Bears and Wolves, only from places she had never been); men who learned to speak the secret dialects of the languages of Grass and Star and Tree, and who translated what they said for everyone to hear and then were hunted by great beasts as a reward; men who walked in one direction for years and years and years until they found the part of the sky that had shattered apart the day the first birds had been born, and who broke off a piece to make a new kind of bird for themselves; men who became dear to Anna—nearly as dear as the Swallow Man himself—men with names like Kepler, like Bohr and Heisenberg and Galileo and Einstein and Copernicus. And Anna's very favorite: grand, imperious Newton and his sweet, backward, bumbling squire, Willy Whiston.

Every several nights, when it had been dark for so long that Anna was afraid it would never be light again, they would crawl out of their little hole of stone and story and visit the town.

Their purpose was simple: stay alive and avoid detection at all costs.

Though they quickly discovered which doors in the town were left unlocked and which pantries were closer to the unlocked doors than they were to their keepers' bedrooms, often they would have to pass over this low-hanging fruit so as to keep from being known.

It was, nonetheless, this winter that, in defiance of all good reason, the Swallow Man opened a low window and climbed through to fetch Anna a thick slice of the *babka* that had been sitting on the counter as they passed.

In truth, there was only so much they could do about their footprints in the snow. Entering or exiting the town, they kept on the road, and from there, there was no real problem. Even if it was snowing in the dead of night when they visited, they could easily keep to the street and their footprints would be lost by morning. On the one or two occasions that they encountered a fresh, new blanket of snow in the town with no more falling, they simply took care and brushed their tracks out behind them with a pine branch where they led to and from the road.

It was in the trees that the problem came about. Moving between the road and the forest was easy enough—a brook cut beneath a little bridge where it met the road just a few minutes' walk in the wrong direction, and as long as they didn't spend too much time wetting their shoes, they could easily get in and out of the forest without leaving a trail. In the forest itself, however, there were few options. The trees were not sturdy enough or close enough together that they could climb one to another to make their way through the canopy, and finally they had simply to resign themselves to leaving tracks in the deeper forest, where (as much as any one place in the world) it could be said that they lived.

They had done about as well as could've been expected—there was no trail to lead anyone from the missing food back to the forest.

In the end, though, no amount of caution could have kept them safe there.

Aside from telling stories, the dominant occupation of time in their little stone hole was napping. An excellent pastime and assuager of hunger pangs, it had the added benefit of keeping them rested up for their nocturnal excursions into town.

The Swallow Man often left for short walks around the immediate area while Anna dozed. He was always there when she closed her eyes and when she opened them back up again, but she was a very light sleeper, and she nearly always heard the crunch of his boots in the snow as he left.

Anna didn't walk when the Swallow Man slept. She liked to watch him. His face in sleep reminded her of the Swallow Man he became when they visited the wetlands. Perhaps it was only the memory of their first night in the hills outside of Kraków, but watching him in that state, witnessing his even, measured sleeping breath, she always felt as if she were closer to seeing into who, precisely, he was.

It was dark when Anna awoke that night. It was the feet first, crunching the snow, just as the Swallow Man's had done when he'd left, only now there were more, many, many feet more, and metal brushing lightly against metal with the movement of bodies.

The Swallow Man had not returned. Out beyond the rocks it was dark. A few voices murmured as the feet tramped by her, but Anna couldn't make out any specific words or language. She held her breath.

They had passed her by when it started. She could still hear their feet in the snow, but they were a ways off now, not so near that she feared to breathe.

The first gunshot was single, from a handgun or rifle, and then there was the sound of a woman screaming.

There is no way to properly describe this sort of screaming to a person who has never heard it. It's a sound somehow beyond the limitations of the body that produces it, so harsh and sharp as to seem almost otherworldly, but so animal as to produce in your witnessing body a sort of shadow scream that echoes violently around the inside of your chest. The word for it is not "distress," or "horror." Really, there is not an adequate word in any language. The only way to imagine the sound of that sort of screaming is to think of it as the sound produced when the universe rips itself open to let Death come through.

It was only one person screaming at first, then a ripple of muttering, and then raised voices yelling at the mutterers. Still, Anna couldn't make out the language. Dogs began to bark, and then gunshots, more and more, quickly, on the heels of one another, and then the screaming and crying multiplied, spreading outward amongst the voices like a contagion.

Someone was laughing.

By the end the only sounds were gunshots. They tapered off, until at last there were only intermittent spurts, two or three at a time, correcting any residual life that had been left behind.

Anna was gripping so hard with her throat, her hand

clapped over her mouth, to keep herself from making any noise that she thought her head would burst. Her face, her jaw, her throat, her eyes, all pounded from the squeezing tension. She wanted so badly not to be crying, but she couldn't stop.

Anna could hear the soldiers' boots and their idle conversation tracking back toward her, could smell cigarette smoke stronger and stronger as they approached. The dogs' collars clinked lightly against their leads.

"Frightened" does not describe how she felt. Fright is an uncertainty. She was certain that she would shortly die.

Her footprints were all over the area, and the Swallow Man's, too, and each set led either to or from the place where she was sitting at that very moment.

These Bears or Wolves, these animals, they would sniff her out and come and find her, for certain. She was alone.

She would be found.

Her mind raced madly, but she couldn't think of a name to call herself in order to stop them from hurting her, and she had no berries, and outside of her hole, so very near, one of them was laughing. She had followed, as best as she had been able, all the rules and principles and systems that the Swallow Man had laid in place, but no matter how much planning and logic one arms oneself with against the world, still the snow falls, and still your feet mark tracks behind you where you go.

No amount of theory could have saved her.

And then she heard it. Somewhere, nearby:

The swallow's song.

Perhaps it was impossible that she would survive, but

hearing the song of a bird sung by a man—this introduced to her mind the forgotten notion that impossible things could exist in the world.

What had kept her alive until now was not rules—it was the Swallow Man.

And the Swallow Man was singing.

If they had been looking when they first arrived, it is quite likely that the soldiers would've seen the footprints dotting the area, but their prey had gone ahead of them and wiped the tracks into oblivion with their own trudging feet. Perhaps one or two amongst the fallen had seen the footprints—perhaps had even understood what they meant. But that was no danger anymore.

The soldiers left after a brief quarter of an hour, but the Swallow Man didn't come and get Anna until the morning.

They left directly, without speaking.

Anna didn't look at the twenty or so empty bodies as they passed by. Instead, she looked at the spent shell casings.

Several months earlier, in the autumn of the eastern part of the country, Anna and the Swallow Man had come upon a tree to which someone had tacked a church ikon. She had seen trees with bits of their bark stripped off before, and to her it seemed entirely natural that, in that season, one of those great trees that rained down leaves of red and brown and gold would be hiding such a brilliant, colorful picture beneath its skin. She went over for a closer look, to pull back more of the bark in order to see the parts of the picture that remained hidden, but something else caught her eye—around the foot of the tree there was a litter of small, cylindrical, brass-colored things. They were cold in her palm and smelled vaguely of smoke, and she tucked one of them into the pocket of her dress to take with her. It followed that a peculiar tree with pictures beneath its bark might very well bear peculiar nuts. In fact, this was so intuitive that she didn't even think to ask the Swallow Man about it.

But when Anna saw the shells here amongst the bodies of the dead, she knew instantly that they didn't belong to nuts.

She dropped the one she'd picked up, still riding in her pocket, down into the snow.

Now she knew what rifles did.


It was something like six months later when Anna met a man in the woods who was kissing his rifle.

The Swallow Man was close to running out of his pills, and beyond question he needed to find more. By this point he no longer hid the ritual of their consumption from Anna, in the morning, afternoon, and evening, but neither did he tell her why he was leaving her alone in the forest when he went into Lublin. Of course she knew, and of course he knew that she knew. He made no effort to disguise the dwindling number of pills in his flask every day. But some secrets, though widely known, are better kept hidden away.

There was a complex calculus that determined whether it was safer to leave Anna in the forest or take her into the city, and the value of many of the variables in the equation was left to speculation.

Anyone could see that things were changing, worsening in the cities—this was the high period of the ghettos—but to what extent this might affect Anna and the Swallow Man should they venture into the jumbled tangle of rusty, barbed city chaos was not clear.

Whether he was alone or accompanied, it was a delicate thing the Swallow Man had to do, to appear so unassailably authoritative that people feared to look him in the eye. Being accompanied by little girls tends to humanize great men, and there was nothing the Swallow Man wanted less in that moment than humanization.

They'd never spoken of the winter massacre, simply moved on with their lives and found a place to finish out the winter before setting off again at its end, and that day in the trees, watching him walk away from her, tall and spindly, the bag hanging down from his bough of an arm, Anna wanted to say something about it for the first time. She didn't like being without the Swallow Man. She didn't like to remember that she'd forgotten about him, even for a moment. It gave her an old, familiar pain in her fingertips, as if they were trying to rip through cold, rusty metal.

But no words came, and soon he was gone between the thin trees.

There was little for Anna to do but wait. She sat down on the soft forest floor, adept now at maneuvering herself into a place of comfort between the tree roots, and pulled, with quiet gratitude, the small pair of leather shoes from her pinched, pained feet.

She wiggled her tingling toes in the warm breeze, and she sighed. The day was unreservedly beautiful.

It has always been a mystery how it is possible that in the midst of great horror, the weather can continue on so obliviously warm and bright and lovely. Horrors were not few on that day, not even so very far from where Anna sat. But the sunlight never seemed to know, and thank God for it. If there had been no sunlight behind the thin green leaves in the wilds of Poland, Anna Łania might have had no understanding at all of why it was not good to die.

The man came crashing through the trees, so loudly she thought he must've been making a joke.

He was not too tall—broad, but not stocky—and his beard was full and on the long side. Beneath his round, boxy cap, his hair was close-cropped. To Anna he registered simply as a grown-up, but he could hardly have been past his twenties or, at best, the shallow end of his thirties.

Most fascinating and terrifying to her, though, was the rifle slung over his shoulder. By that time Anna had seen an endless array of personal weapons: automatic, semiautomatic, bolt-action, of all makes and origins and colorations, with varying degrees of wear. What that man was carrying, though, was a weapon she had never seen.

Some soldiers had fine leather shoulder straps for their rifles; others, simpler cloth arrangements; and still others chose to carry their weapons in the crooks of their arms, like children. This was the first time Anna had seen a rifle held in place with shoelaces. Around his feet the tongues of the young man's boots flapped and wagged as his heels came unseated with each step.

And what manner of soldier was this? He wore no uniform, seemed to have no regard whatsoever for his feet. . . . He was acting very strangely, and his weapon was terribly odd.

The wood of the thing was dark, nearly black. That in and of itself was not so out of the ordinary as to raise Anna's curiosity—guns came in all colors—but the fittings to this man's looked like silver, and her eyes could find no triggering mechanism. How would she know when it was necessary to become frightened if she couldn't see when he was preparing to shoot?

The shape of the gun itself was the main irregularity. Where most rifles had a long, thin barrel coming off of a thicker stock that grew back into a butt shaped for bracing against the shoulder, this one was cylindrical for nearly the entire span of its length. The muzzle tapered into a wedging, rounded point, and down near the bottom, where the butt ought to have been, it flared out like the end of a bell.

The young man took a drink from the glass bottle in his hand and sat roughly down on the trunk of a fallen tree. If Anna had known what drunkenness was, she would certainly have had no trouble in recognizing it.

Her fascination only grew when the young man lifted the rifle to his lips.

What was he doing? This was entirely wrong. Anna was not a soldier herself, of course, had never learned the protocols and regulations of any military, but she prided herself on her understanding of the importance of rules and systems and grammars and standards—the Swallow Man himself, after all, was half man and half command—and everything about this strange new fellow seemed to be a gross violation of The Rules.

The young man closed his eyes, and holding the narrow end of his rifle in his mouth, he breathed in deeply through his nose.

There was a question germinating inside Anna's chest, a question too large to be bounded in by language—the question of the young man himself—and before she could stop herself, words came tumbling forth out of her mouth.

"What are you doing?"

The moment she spoke, Anna knew it had been wrong. Instinctively she clapped one hand over her mouth, and just as quickly she dropped it again, the Swallow Man's teaching echoing in her head:

*Regret is like golden jewelry: at the proper moment it may prove immeasurably valuable, but it is rarely wise to advertise its presence to strangers.*

Fortunately, the young man had missed her momentary show of regret entirely; in his bewilderment at Anna's sudden voice, he had jumped and fallen backward off of his tree-trunk seat.

"Oh my . . ." The fear in his eyes as he turned to look at Anna was completely and utterly transparent. She was unaccustomed to people in the woods who became frightened and made no attempt to hide it.

Everything about this man was strange.

"*Riboyno shel oylum!* Just a little girl," he said, dusting himself off and repairing to his tree trunk. "You scared me!"

Anna was not terribly pleased to be called "just" anything, but she was too curious to allow herself to become distracted. "What kind of rifle is that?"

The young man wheeled about furiously, looking directly behind himself and then, somehow staggeringly despite his seated position, in every other conceivable direction. "What? Where?"

"Your rifle. What kind is it? Why were you kissing it?"

The young man stared at Anna, wide-eyed, red-faced, and sweating, brow wrinkled in incomprehension for a long moment.

And then he started to laugh.

This man's laughter was, to Anna, wonderfully instructive. The Swallow Man was truly a great man, and his life was beautiful, but he guarded his laughter jealously—he had given none in close to two years—and in her childhood there had been so much laughter that was the laughter of one person exalting over another. This young man, though, he laughed for joy and for relief. He laughed because things were not as bad as they might've been. He laughed easily, and he laughed well.

"Oh, darling girl, no!" he said. "No! This is not a rifle! This is a clarinet!"

"What's a clarinet?"

He raised his eyebrows. "A clarinet is a musical instrument. Like me."

In Yiddish both the instrument and the player are called *klei-zemer*—or *klezmer.*

Anna frowned.

"What," said the young man. "You don't know music?"

She did. Anna knew the word, and she knew the experience, but she hadn't heard any in a very long time.

"I *remember* music," said Anna. "I just don't *know* any." She had become accustomed, in the Swallow Man's company, to forgoing desires. It had been a very long time since she had asked for anything she wanted, and there was a dangerous, transgressive pleasure in asking now. "Can you play for me, Reb Clarinet?"

Reb Clarinet smiled at this from behind his thick brown beard, his apple cheeks rising toward his eyes.

"This," he said, hoisting his instrument, "is a clarinet. I am Hirschl."

This could not have been less interesting to Anna. "All right. Can you play for me, Reb Hirschl?"

Reb Hirschl's face fell. "Oh. No, I'm very sorry. I can't, Miss . . . uh . . . Miss . . . What's your name?"

Perhaps it was the sudden absence of his beautiful mirth, or perhaps it was the inquiry itself, but with a jolt a bright, stark light came on in Anna's head. She didn't have a name. She couldn't have a name. And here this man threw his about like it was nothing. She could feel the dangerous, easy joy of this odd, fabulous, intoxicating man like a warm, sweet deluge beginning to sweep her off her guard. She struggled to want to resist.

He was looking at her, waiting. What was her name? His

round red cheeks drew her eye irresistibly, and the vocabulary of Road names she had collected slipped and squirmed around in her mind, evading capture.

After a moment's stutter she gave up and changed the subject. "But why can't you play?"

This question brought Reb Hirschl sadness again, and Anna felt immediately sorry. She liked the way Reb Hirschl looked. His shoulders were square, and she wanted to put her palm against his chest and feel it rise and fall and vibrate with his speech, almost as much when he was happy as when he was sad.

"Because," he said, "my last reed is cracked." He reached down into the grubby sock on his right foot and pulled out a strip of yellowish cane, rounded at the top. There was a clear crack running down the grain, through which the sunlight shone.

Anna cocked her head to the right in inquiry, as she had seen the Swallow Man do so many times. "What does that mean? What's a reed?"

"Well," said Reb Hirschl, tucking his reed back into his sock, "if a clarinet is like a rifle, which it isn't, and if the notes of music are like the things a rifle shoots, which they aren't, then the reed is like the cartridge, you know, the magazine you put into the gun to make it shoot. It makes it work. When it vibrates—like your throat when you speak—sound comes out of it. If there's no reed, there's no sound."

"So really, the *reed's* the instrument. Not you or the clarinet."

"In a way," said Reb Hirschl. "If it's cracked, then the sound won't be any good."

"But there'll be sound?"

He frowned and bobbed his head back and forth in equivocation. "Sure," he said. "Some."

"Well, then why don't you play it?"

"Because the sound won't be as good as if it *wasn't* cracked. And if I play on it, the crack will get worse."

This made absolutely no sense to Anna. "But if you *don't* play on it, there'll be no music at *all*."

Reb Hirschl frowned and nodded. "This is true."

"So will you play?"

Reb Hirschl shook his head. "No. I can't risk ruining the reed."

Anna was incredulous. This was nonsense.

"But," said Reb Hirschl, "I'll do what I was about to do when you stopped me."

"What's that?"

"I was going to practice. All the fingerings and everything, only instead of blowing, I was just going to hum."

"What?"

For a moment Reb Hirschl looked as if he were going to try to explain again, but then he sighed. "Just listen."

Reb Hirschl put the reedless clarinet in his mouth, closed his eyes, breathed in deep through his nose, and began to hum. The sound of his voice coming through the instrument was odd and muffled, and his fingers clacked on the stops and catches of the thing in a strange way, but through it all Anna could hear the music in him.

His was a dark and soft and round voice, and on it he played a sweet, mournful doina.

He played and he played, simply at first, and low, but soon rising and climbing, and every so often Anna looked up and saw him, eyes pressed closed, swaying gently, walking deeper into his music.

There was a moment in which she knew that if she didn't stand up and sneak off now, she would not be able to later, but this prospect was not entirely unpleasant, and she had already made up her mind.

Finally she leaned her back up against the trunk of his tree and closed her eyes like him, that she might be able to hear the music the way he did.

This is how Anna fell in love with the man who kissed his rifle.

Anna saw it, but Reb Hirschl did not. The Swallow Man had his knife in his hand.

If her eyes had not been closed like his, Anna might've seen the Swallow Man coming. She might've been able to catch his eyes and show him without speaking that everything was all right. Things might've been different from the very beginning.

As it was, the Swallow Man had made a small noise, a rustle in the brush, the snap of a twig, and both Anna's eyes and the Jew's had flown open. Anna knew perfectly well that this was a sign of their relative safety from the Swallow Man—had he wanted, he could easily have come upon both of them silently with his knife, and, eyes pressed closed to better hear the music, neither of them would've known until they felt the blade.

But Reb Hirschl was aware of none of this.

Despite his inebriation and his flapping boots, he was on his feet before Anna. With his right hand he held his clarinet by his side, parallel to the ground, and with his left he drew Anna in and sheltered her behind his leg.

The Swallow Man had gathered Anna close on more than one occasion, but to put himself between her and danger—this was not something that the Swallow Man would've done.

"Well," said Reb Hirschl. "This is a popular corner of the woods today." There was a chuckle in his voice, light and re-assuring, inoffensive. Friendly. This, too, was a departure from what Anna knew. Despite the Swallow Man's skill in turning strangers into compatriots, he himself was never friendly. Friendly was an extension of self. Friendly was easily rebuffed.

Friendly was weak.

The Swallow Man did not speak at first. There was a perfect stillness to him in that moment that seemed terribly danger-ous. He simply looked. And then, finally, he turned his gaze from Reb Hirschl's face down to Anna's.

"Are you all right, Sweetie?"

He extended his long-fingered hand—the right, palm up-ward.

Anna knew that he favored his left hand, the hand that hung down by his side, its back facing out, concealing the unendingly sharpened knife blade like a scythe amongst the boughs of his fingers. She felt no choice in the matter but to work herself free of Reb Hirschl and go to take the Swallow Man's waiting hand.

Looking at Reb Hirschl from the opposite side of the

situation was a jarring experience. It was viscerally frightening to see the Swallow Man across from you, still and silent, waiting, ready. To see Reb Hirschl in the late-spring sunlight was almost laughable. His round, boxy cap was off-center on his close-shorn, perfectly round head, his beard was thick and unruly, his clothes unkempt, and his boots only a moment or two from coming off. He swayed slightly on his feet, like the trees in the breeze. His clarinet hung loose in his fingertips.

He didn't even have a reed for the thing.

With the authority and implacability that only a nine-year-old can have in rendering such judgments, Anna found herself thinking how childish he looked.

There was a moment of alarm and disappointment, and sadness, almost betrayal, in his face when she went to the Swallow Man, and then in his slow, hazy eyes she saw understanding.

"Oh," he said. "You must be—"

"Daddy," Anna said. She hoped that her unprompted return to the riverbank might mitigate the danger that she felt creeping through the Swallow Man's hard finger bones where they wrapped around her wrist, but the Swallow Man did not relax.

A light of real, genuine relief lit in Reb Hirschl's eyes. Anna could see him beginning to reach his hand out to shake her daddy's when the Swallow Man spoke.

"Thank you," he said, and the words seemed sudden, like the quick clearing of an unseen throat in the darkness. "For looking after her."

His hands did not stir, and Reb Hirschl abandoned his intended handshake before his arm could even fully extend. "Ah," he said. "It was no trouble at all."

This was a first in Anna's travels with the Swallow Man. Reb Hirschl was extending himself in kindness, and the Swallow Man was rebuffing him. At every turn the Swallow Man had espoused and incarnated a very simple philosophy that relied upon the idea that one needn't suffer to give benefit to another person, that the connections between people, however brief, however ephemeral, however false, even, had the very real potential to save us all.

And here he was, doing his best to drive someone away.

"Daddy," said Anna. "This is Reb Hirschl."

Reb Hirschl inclined his head. "A pleasure."

The Swallow Man did not answer him. "Sweetie," he said, "are you ready to go?"

There was only one answer to this question. The Swallow Man knew it, Anna knew it, and even poor Reb Hirschl knew it.

"Yes," she said. "I'm ready."


Anna and the Swallow Man moved through the trees, silent, side by side, away from the place where they had met Reb Hirschl the Jew, walking just as they always had. Only for Anna it was nothing like it had been before.

There were many things Anna was unsure of. She didn't know very well how life was supposed to work under normal circumstances. She didn't even know what normal circumstances *were*, really, or what things like "real" or "fake" meant.

She certainly didn't understand the boundaries that people wrapped around others in their different varieties—the Swallow Man and she crossed these borders as easily as they breathed. In fact, if Anna and the Swallow Man could have been called any one thing, in the way that some people are called farmers or cobblers or milkmen, they would've been called crossers-over. And yet, for the life of her, she couldn't see how they weren't walking away from Reb Hirschl because of the borders and boundaries that other men had drawn around him.

"Because he's a Jew?" Anna asked. This was the first thing either of them had said since they had left Reb Hirschl behind.

"For a lot of reasons," said the Swallow Man. He did not look at Anna.

"Is one of them that he's a Jew?"

"Yes." The Swallow Man was unapologetic. "There are some ways of being that are more dangerous than others right now, and the Jewish way is one of the worst."

"But I like him."

Anna thought for sure that this would compel the Swallow Man to stop and turn to face her, as he had done so often in the early days of their travel, but he did not stop. He did not even turn his head.

"I know you like him," said the Swallow Man. "But we are not chasing after things that we like. We are chasing after our lives. We are trying to earn our survival."

"Why ours and not his?"

"Because we are us and he is not. The world is at war."

"Are we at war?"

It took the Swallow Man a moment to answer, but it was not a very long moment. "Yes," he said.

"On whom? On him?"

"No. Not on anyone. *For* ourselves."

She tried as best she could, but Anna couldn't see how you could be at war without someone to fight against.

"But if we're at war for ourselves . . . does that mean we're at war on . . . everyone else?"

This made the Swallow Man stop and face her, and in Anna's aching little chest, this attention felt like a distinct victory, until she heard what he had to say.

"Sweetie," said the Swallow Man. "Anna—yes."

Anna frowned. This did not seem right. "But what about the other people? The people that we like?"

"Like whom?"

"Like Reb Hirschl."

"I don't like Reb Hirschl the way that you do."

This felt like avoidance—a technicality. "Well," said Anna, "you must like *some*one."

"I like you."

"That doesn't count. 'You' is just a way of saying 'me' in Road."

Despite himself, the Swallow Man smiled at this. He did not answer, but Anna was not done with the conversation. "But, Swallow Man?"

"Yes?"

"You do like people. What about all our friends? The ones

that we met on the road? You liked them. They always helped us and gave us nice things."

"Yes," said the Swallow Man.

"Well, why did we never give *them* any nice things?"

"Because," said the Swallow Man. "A friend is not someone to whom you give the things that you need when the world is at war. A friend is someone to whom you give the things that you need when the world is at peace. And unlike 'you,' Sweetie, 'friend' is not Road for 'me.'"

This, troublingly, Anna understood. She knew that she wanted to live, and she knew that she wanted the Swallow Man to live in the same way. More than she wanted others, even nice others, to live.

But she also knew that she didn't want poor, foolish, silly, beautiful Reb Hirschl to die. He was other people. But he didn't have to be. And maybe Anna didn't want him to be.

She wasn't sure how to express this—it felt like a question she wanted to ask, but she couldn't discover the words to wrap around it to make it askable. Besides, the Swallow Man listened to her, and he gave real consideration to the things she said, but once his mind was made up, she had never known him to reverse a decision. Reb Hirschl was dangerous, he would say. In many ways.

With this, Anna could not argue. She understood this instinctively.

And so the matter lapsed.

But Anna did not forget.

Lublin was one of the largest cities in eastern Poland, and

the Swallow Man had a policy of not lingering in the vicinity of such places any longer than he had to. He would not even stop to change his clothes until they had put a great distance between themselves and that deadly jumble of brick and flesh, and they moved swiftly that afternoon to pass beyond the radius of its danger.

Many things called Anna's attention that day, and by the time the residual light of the sky began to hurry to catch up with the sun where it had fallen beyond the horizon, her mind had gone through many occupations: her aching feet; the heel of bread that the Swallow Man had saved in his physician's bag, and whether tonight would be the night for its consumption; various small sights of beauty, which she had learned to hide away about herself like a squirrel, in the knowledge that the desolation of winter was always on the way. At one point the Swallow Man had given her a thorough lesson on the mysteries of symbiotic fungi, which she had found, as always when he waxed instructive, quite interesting. But the room of each of these ideas, no matter how large or small, was never empty when she came into it.

No matter where in her mind she wandered, Anna found Reb Hirschl there.

She wondered where he would sleep that night.

She wondered if uncracked reeds were common or rare.

She wondered where he was going—by now she knew that almost no one had so nebulous a destination as the Swallow Man and she—and she wondered what he would do when he got there.

More than anything, though, she did not wonder. She simply saw him in her mind—his abashing round red cheeks, his thorough chest, his rough, blocky hands lifting his clarinet with delicate care. And she heard his warm voice.

Anna and the Swallow Man rarely lit fires, even in the colder months. They almost never ate food that required cooking, and though the warmth would often have been welcome, the attendant light and the notice a fire drew were almost never a worthwhile sacrifice. As a result—particularly in the summer months, when the nights are brief—they often lay down to sleep directly at the coming of darkness.

That night they stopped at a hedgerow that delineated the border between one farmer's pasture and the next, and after they ate (that night was not, unfortunately, the night for bread), they settled in beneath it to sleep.

The Swallow Man, as was his way, simply rolled over and remained still, but Anna could not find the quietude of mind necessary for her own rest.

Normally, her mind was like a busy beach—all day long she would run back and forth, leaving footprints, building small mounds and castles, writing out ideas and diagrams with her fingers in the sand, but when the night tide came in, she would close her eyes and allow each wave of rhythmic breath to wash in and out over her day's accumulation, and before long the beach would be clear and empty, and she would drift out to sleep.

But tonight, silhouetted in the moonlight, a man stood on her beach. The tide of her breath rose and washed around his ankles, but still Reb Hirschl stood there, unmoving, and she could not make herself sleep. She tossed and she turned, but nothing she did could shake him loose from the place where he stood.

*Go to sleep.*

The problem was that there were so many elementary things that the Jew clearly did not understand. She knew intimately the feeling of insufficient shoes, and his seemed as if they might've fit rather well if he hadn't madly chosen to pull out the laces. It was impossible that he understood the grave consequences he was tempting. Furthermore, he had given his name up with such careless largesse—without concern, as if it cost him nothing. Slowed as he must've been by his flapping shoes, throwing his name out onto the wind as if he were sowing seed—in no time he would be found. It was a surety. And Anna knew what it meant to be found.

*Go to sleep.*

That was assuming he didn't simply stumble into trouble, which was more than likely. He'd been completely unaware of Anna when he tramped into the clearing that day, and she hadn't even been putting forth any effort at hiding herself. Did he know the utility and the danger of roads and paths? It seemed clear that he did not. Likely, he would simply continue tromping aimlessly on until he ran into one of the many thousands of things in the world that could stop people from moving.

He was like an old blind man in the middle of a vast thicket of angry iron thorns.

*Go to sleep.*

But even if, miraculously, he managed to avoid all these snares, it was more than likely that he would waste away and die in the short term anyway. It was plain to see that he had no knowledge of the country, no expertise in roots and plants, and no one was very likely to give of their precious stock of food to a bumbling Jew these days. Even with skill and cunning, Anna and the Swallow Man often went for an exceedingly long time without the sort of stuff common to larders and pantries and other vaults of cultivated human food. What were his chances? Nil.

*Just go to sleep.*

In point of fact, she had not seen that Reb Hirschl had been carrying anything at all about him, excepting his clarinet and his small bottle. He was undoubtedly hungry now. How likely was it that he had eaten in the past day? And food was the one indulgence she knew could draw a person forward through the pain of ill-shod walking. In fact, she herself would very likely not have been able to make it through today's progress if she had not had the memory of that heel of bread in the Swallow Man's bag to chase after.

Forgetting even the real thing itself, would poor Reb Hirschl ever taste the *anticipation* of bread again before, as was practically inevitable, he was wiped carelessly out of the world?

The answer to this question was clear, and it weighed Anna down so heavily that no breath, no matter how steady, could ever hope to wash her out to sleep.

And so she opened her eyes and sat up.


Anna did not so much make a decision as understand what it was that she was going to do.

The Swallow Man was curled up around his physician's bag, facing in toward the hedgerow, but fortunately Anna was nimble, and the Swallow Man's umbrella had fallen from its accustomed place atop the bag. All she had to do was open the clasp and take the bread.

Before long she had the heel of bread in her hand. It seemed awfully small now, smaller than she had remembered, but this was mainly by comparison with the massive idea of Reb Hirschl in her mind. For a tiny moment she wondered if the task she had set for herself was even worth the effort for so insufficient a quantity of comfort.

But the life she had built with the Swallow Man was an existence predicated on the value of insufficiencies. Anything was always better than nothing.

And so, re-creating as best she could the opposite of their arrival trajectory, Anna set out away from the hedgerow to find Reb Hirschl the Jew.

If she had stopped to think, she would've known that what she was attempting was a thing of terrible risk, that it fiercely violated the Swallow Man's principles, that she was tempting harm upon herself, and even that the likelihood of her success was ludicrously small—all of these things were well within the grasp of her mind.

But it is the peculiar talent of a child to exist in perfect comfort and happiness entirely without the burden of forethought. All she knew was that out there, in a place in the woods near Lublin, there was a beautiful man to whom she wanted to give the taste of bread one final time before he died.

Anna spent quite a while trying to recover the woods, and when she turned around to check that she was still moving away from the hedgerow at the proper angle, she had wandered far from its sight. The only things around her were grass and field and hill, and when she finally stilled her frantic scanning of the horizon, she had lost her sense of direction entirely.

There is no labyrinth as treacherous as that with neither paths nor walls.

Anna was immediately terrified. Never before had she felt lost moving in the forests and plains, because never before had she done so without the Swallow Man, but now she could no more point herself in his direction than she could in Reb Hirschl's.

But she knew the Swallow Man's dictum. *You can be found if you stay still, and to be found is the greatest danger. Better lost than found.*

Anna chose a direction and began to walk.

But now she was frightened, and there is no greater explicator of one's own mistakes than sudden fear.

If you could be found if you stayed still, did it not follow that if you moved, you could *not* be found? This was why she herself was walking. Why was it at all likely that Reb Hirschl would not have moved? Anna and the Swallow Man had covered much ground since they met the Jew—who was to say that he had not also? And even if she managed to find Reb Hirschl, how would they make their way back to the Swallow Man?

And what if she were to come upon Reb Hirschl in the midst of trouble? It was clear that he would not stay out of it for long. How might she save him from what threatened? Surely, the

Swallow Man might've invented some sort of plot or method to help him, and she might've contributed somehow, in her way, but she could not imagine what she might do if a Bear or a Wolf leveled his rifle at her poor, sweet, beautiful Reb Hirschl.

When the trees of the woods came into view, darkening the horizon, Anna seized on them like a piece of happy news. Surely, they were the same trees out of which she and the Swallow Man had come earlier that day. Surely, she was on the right track. The direction forward was ahead, and the direction back was behind.

In vain security Anna clutched her bit of bread to her chest, tried to stir up a smile, and trotted forward toward the trees.

At first she attacked the woods with urgency, moving swiftly through the thick ranks of trees. Of necessity, though, she began slowly to correct her course by tiny degrees in order to move around brush and trunk, and before long she realized how great a challenge it was to maintain a straight direction of travel in a pathless forest. She had not bothered to note the position of the moon or stars when she'd ducked beneath the lowest branches, but even if she had, the canopy was so thick here that there could be no help for her above. Almost no light filtered down to her. She could not clearly see what lay ahead of her, or behind, or to either side. She attempted to set her feet quietly down, one after the other, but she often could not clearly see what lay beneath her, either, and frequently she would tread on a root or a fallen branch, and her clumsy noise would seem to fill the forest.

Anna tried not to think about how obvious she must've been to things with nighttime eyes and thick jaws.

Each further step was a terror.

Each breath was a loud, echoing betrayal.

On the wind she could smell burning and smoke. She wanted to get back out of the trees, would've settled for simply returning to the hedgerow and abandoning her goal if she could be back in a safe place, but even this was impossible now. Back was as obscure as forth.

Anna stopped and sat down on the ground. A part of her longed to think that perhaps she could just stay here, simply sit and be safe until the rising of the sun, but another part, just as large, questioned if the sun ever rose in these dark woods.

And then, behind her and to the left, something moved.

Anna was on her feet and running before she had time to think. Nothing is so terrifying as unexpected motion in the dark, and now she could hear, coming swiftly after her, feet falling in easy, loping pursuit. With everything she had, Anna battled away forward, but she could not escape the sound of the long legs that seemed to box her in wherever she turned. She ran as hard as she could, holding one hand out in front of her to ward off the branches that clawed at her face, wishing beyond hope for some sort of salvation to swoop down from the canopy and carry her away before thick, sharp teeth penetrated her skin at the shoulder or heel, but her foot caught on something unseen, and she stumbled, clutching the bread close to her chest, her fingers cutting into its stale crumb, and fell hard onto the ground.

As she crashed down, the sound of nimble feet behind her fell silent.

In the sudden still, she heard, far off, muted laughter, the plucking of a stringed instrument, song. The smell of burning was stronger here, and with a surge Anna's heart filled with hope. *People. There must be people near.*

*Human beings are the best hope in the world of other human beings to survive.*

Far off, beyond the trees, she thought she could see the vague orange glow of fire, and she pushed herself to her feet and made to run again when she heard a voice.

"Anna," it said, and her heart froze solid like winter earth.

Then, between the trees, a match flame flared into tiny life, and in the sudden illumination far above her, Anna saw the dark countenance of the Swallow Man.

"Anna," he said. "Stop."


The last thing Anna wanted to do was cry. Every muscle in her face ached.

"Where were you going?" The match light flickered beneath the empty face of the Swallow Man and threatened at every moment to go out. Anna would much have preferred that he raise his voice for once, that he yell and storm, but when he spoke again, his intonation was as even and measured as it had been the first time.

"Where were you going?"

Anna didn't answer.

Just as the Swallow Man extended his long, open, empty hand in front of her, the match flame in his other guttered and died in a tiny plume of smoke. She put the heel of bread into the Swallow Man's hand, and in the silent darkness she began to cry.

"Will you tell me," said the Swallow Man in the dark for the third time, "where you were going?"

Anna did her best to keep the sound of tears from her voice, straining to keep hers as balanced as the Swallow Man's had been. "Don't you know?"

"Of course I know," said the Swallow Man. "But I need you to tell me."

This seemed like cruelty to Anna.

"Why?" she said, her voice erring far too close for her liking to the wobble of distress.

"Because," said the Swallow Man, "I need to know if you thought you were going back toward the Jew, or if you thought you were going away from me."

If Anna had been able to see the Swallow Man's impassive face, she might not have felt so viscerally the force of sadness in this question. She had not thought how the Swallow Man might feel to wake and see her gone, but this was not a particular omission. She had not thought in general.

"I was not going away from you," she said, and for all her effort, her distress deepened at the thought that the Swallow Man might have even considered this possibility. "I was not."

"Ah," said the unseen Swallow Man, "but you were. No matter what you meant to do, the distinction exists only in words. Toward him is the same as away from me. It is only by a trick of language that we may say one and not the other."

Anna wanted to protest, but she could not still her tears long enough.

"Do you understand me?"

Anna could not answer.

For a moment the Swallow Man allowed her to cry in silence, and then he spoke.

"Anna," said the Swallow Man. "If I wake up and you have gone away from me again, you will not find me. I will make certain of it. Do you understand that?"

The darkness was impenetrably thick, but forgetting herself, Anna nodded vigorously. She would've said that she was sorry—she was—but her voice threatened to detonate into shrapnel if she let it loose.

A tiny sigh entered into the world from the direction of the Swallow Man, far above her, and he said, "Tell me *why* you went."

The corner of the darkness where the Swallow Man was hidden felt so taut to Anna in its quiet that she was afraid it might rip open.

Somewhere she could hear men singing together.

The Swallow Man's inquiry seemed cruel, and unfair—like a trap. He knew where she had been going. Didn't he know, then, why? Couldn't he guess, he who knew where to find every sustaining thing in the world, how to pass by every threat in safety, he who carried wisdom in one hand and danger in the other—how could he possibly *not* know? And if he knew all of this, what use was there in asking her?

Anna was not sure if the Swallow Man spoke again or if it was the warm breeze of the night that whispered *Why?* up above her. She tried to restrain herself, tried to keep calm, but as soon as she opened her mouth, her tears redoubled.

"Why?" Her voice trembled at first, and soon she was sobbing. "Why? I thought you knew! Because he is good and kind and foolish! Because he is alone, and doesn't know enough to be afraid! Because I still see his face and chest and hands when he's gone from me! Because he knows how to laugh, Swallow Man! Because he is not like you!"

A moment of ringing silence chased this explosion, but this silence was not tight like a tensed muscle—it was desolate.

And then: "Yes," said the Swallow Man. "I see."

Almost without meaning to, Anna let a small aftershock roll out of her into the darkness. "Don't say you see unless you really do."

Anna heard the Swallow Man breathe out through his nose. "I do," he said in certainty, and despite her frustration and anger, she could not help believing him for the threadbare, weary quality in his voice.

Anna's crying did not abate as the Swallow Man walked her gently out of the trees and into the soft moonlight. Together they walked across an unfamiliar field at a small distance from one another. If Anna had had her wits about her, she might've noticed an unfamiliar aspect in the Swallow Man's gait—a slow quality, somehow diffuse—but as it was, her tears clouded the world around her to near complete obscurity.

Shortly they came to an old wooden fence that cut haphazardly through the pasture. Once it had been white, but all the paint had long since stripped and curled away, and now the wood seemed to have trouble deciding if it was brown or gray. After a short time spent walking along its length, they found a gate. It had been locked fast by ancient hands, and even if they had removed the lock, it was clear that the hinges of the gate would remain rusted shut.

In her tiny, tired, heartbroken chest, Anna wondered to herself what the difference was between such a gate and the rest of the span of fence into which it had been set.

It was at this point, standing with Anna in front of a useless portal in an antique boundary, that the Swallow Man made up his mind.

He lifted Anna easily to the other side of the fence and then, with little trouble, hopped himself over after her.

In short minutes they had arrived at the exact section of hedgerow beneath which they had originally encamped. This was clear because in his haste to pursue Anna, the Swallow Man had neglected to replace his long umbrella atop the physician's bag. It was still there where it had fallen, in precisely the same position, nestled amongst the bush roots.

Exhausted from her midnight march and from the heavy tax of her sobbing, Anna quickly fell into sleep.

Just when the dawn had begun to creep into the great black night, Anna awoke.

She was alone.

No one was near her.

There was no bag and no umbrella to be seen.

Alone beneath the bushes, Anna Łania allowed a heavy tide of tears to wash her back out into empty, oblivious sleep.

# Patterns of Migration

Anna was woken by the sound of something very close to her head. It squeaked and clicked, like an ungreased device of metal, and before she even opened her eyes, her entire body tensed. The Swallow Man had taught her the danger of mechanical noises, and even if he was gone, she still believed with a full heart in the truth of all his teachings. The sound of a machine where it was not expected could well be relied upon to belong to a machine for making deaths.

But then, in the precise position from which the clicking sound had come, Anna heard a bright whistling and a brush of wings, and when she opened her eyes, it was to the sight of a lone starling flitting off across the bright spring green.

It was not this sight, though, that brought her such racking joy.

There, lying in front of her, curled up close in the precise spot from which he had been gone in the night, was her tall, wise, beautiful, terrifying Swallow Man. A shuddering sigh escaped from her lips.

And then she saw: sprawled out beyond the Swallow Man, barely a sixth of him still beneath the hedge, mouth open, left boot hanging from his toes and clarinet clutched in close, was beautiful, happy, bright, loudly snoring Reb Hirschl.

Where last night she had shaken her body so hard with sobbing that she'd thought she would fly apart, now Anna treasured her tears, as if they were a butterfly of deep blue at flight in the small, sunlit jar of her chest.

When finally she turned her head away from the sight of the Jew, she found the Swallow Man awake and watching her. This did not surprise her—she had long since come to the conclusion that every moment of her life would be subject to his observation—but she could scarcely catch hold of enough breath to speak.

"Why?" she almost didn't say.

The Swallow Man pulled himself lithely out from beneath the hedge and arranged himself in a seated position. "Because," he said. "Just as it is impossible to say 'I was going toward the Jew' without saying 'I was going away from you,' so, too, is it impossible to say 'riverbank' without saying 'river.'"

Anna nodded.

"I had lost sight," said the Swallow Man, "of the fact that survival in and of itself is not sufficient to support every life equally."

Anna thought he might have been preparing to apologize, but just then Reb Hirschl choked deafeningly on a noseful of snore and shifted in his sleep.

"God help us," muttered the Swallow Man.

"Thank you," said Anna. "Thank you." It was only her aching cheeks that finally made Anna aware that she was smiling.

The Swallow Man did not answer, but set about preparing himself to depart. He was fully assembled for the day's walking when, almost as an afterthought, he held out the heel of bread. Anna could see where her clutching fingers had dented its flesh in the night.

"Here," he said. "He insisted that you have it."

There was no lack of judgment in this statement, and that was the way Anna preferred it. Just because she wanted Reb Hirschl by her side, it didn't mean she wanted the Swallow Man at all less, or to be at all different.

Reb Hirschl woke slowly and only at the insistence of the Swallow Man, but from the moment his eyelids lifted, so, too, did his apple cheeks.

Anna had never felt such fulsome gratitude from any "thank you" in any language before in her life. Reb Hirschl pronounced the phrase like a prayer, and for half an hour thereafter, Anna could not speak for blushing.


Despite the bond of Anna between them, the Swallow Man and Reb Hirschl proved thoroughly constitutionally averse. There was hardly anything the Jew did that did not seem to offend the Swallow Man's sensibilities.

The Swallow Man favored strong divisions in all things, but most notably in communication: if he was talking, he was talking, and if he was not, he walked in silence. Reb Hirschl, even once sober, walked in a cloud of small noises. He hummed or sang when there was no conversation to be had, or spoke to himself, muttering small phrases in Yiddish or Hebrew, chuckling, sometimes laughing outright as he went, boots flopping off his heels. To Anna this was a delight, but to the Swallow Man it was distasteful at best and frequently became obnoxious. It was no difficulty to see that, in his more mercurial moments, the Swallow Man found Reb Hirschl truly and completely intolerable.

Though the noise was perhaps the most noticeable issue, it was hardly the only way in which the Jew bothered the Swallow Man. Anna and the Swallow Man had become expert in making use of every last scrap and crumb of food that they encountered—a grain of salt dropped in the dirt, an oily residue left on a fingertip—nothing could escape their mouths for long. When Reb Hirschl ate, on the other hand, half of his food stayed in his beard. This would've been forgivable, perhaps, as clumsiness, but when it resulted from such an obvious combination of zeal and carelessness as to prompt him to sing a little ditty about wiping the crumbs away, it began to rankle.

Anna and the Swallow Man had become accustomed to putting food in their bellies twice in a day—once when they rose and once before they lay down—and in the time between they walked without stopping. Now, though, when they awoke each morning (the first notwithstanding), they found Reb Hirschl already risen, praying silently, his body rocking back and forth at the waist, his palms turned very slightly out and up. He prayed like he sang, with his eyes firmly shut, his lips flitting rapidly through the words of his prayers as his breath flowed into him and back out.

Of course, no matter when he got up, there would still be a troubling amount of prayer left to get through before he was done, and there was nothing that the Swallow Man could less abide than idleness when he wanted to be moving. As if this weren't enough, Reb Hirschl insisted on stopping at midday for a second round of prayer. He prayed a third time at night, before sleeping, often left standing in that shut-eyed, muttering posture when Anna nodded off, and if she hadn't known better, she might've thought he stood praying all throughout the night.

But despite this troublesome piety, most of Reb Hirschl's time was not spent praying. It was spent walking.

Reb Hirschl, though, was a decidedly different sort of walker than the Swallow Man. Where the Swallow Man might lecture and instruct while walking, or, as his only alternative, might remain entirely silent, Reb Hirschl had an immense and variable and delightfully erratic range of walking pastimes.

The most common, of course, was song, and before very long he began to teach Anna a few of his little wordless melodies so that she might sing along with him. Her favorite by far was a brief little two-part walking song that Reb Hirschl had devised to loop back on itself. At any point in their progress, she might start it out, and they would sing together, their notes and phrases and pieces interlocking in a harmonizing double melody. This, Anna loved to do so much that she entirely missed the Swallow Man's exasperation at being subjected to the same thirty seconds of music over and over and over again.

In some long stretches Reb Hirschl would devote his time to the invention of the most asinine and puerile puns and riddles for Anna's attention ("Look! Look! If I've *toad* you once, I've *toad* you a thousand times. Look, see? Toads!"), and each one of these would draw a more exaggerated display of protest and disdain from her than the last. She was nonetheless completely, if covertly, delighted by them. The Swallow Man, needless to say, was not.

On some occasions (usually in midafternoon, when they were all at their tiredest and most hungry and were apt to fall into periods of silent trudgery), Reb Hirschl would simply throw back his head, roar at the top of his lungs, and take off chasing after Anna, who would squeal and run away ineffectually until he caught up with her, threw her over his shoulder, and tickled her until her laughter caught in her throat and tears flooded her eyes. Once this was achieved, he would put her, breathless, back down and proceed as if nothing at all had happened.

Perhaps it was simply willfulness that kept the Swallow Man from enjoying these outbursts in any way, but all the same, he winced whenever the sound of their presence echoed out beyond the hills, and often in those days Anna caught him scanning the horizon compulsively for a hint of anyone who might be following.

One final habit of Reb Hirschl's met with the Swallow Man's express disapproval, though he never wasted his energy in combating it—Reb Hirschl drank. Fortunately, there was no great supply of alcohol to be found in the Polish wild, and even if he'd had the stuff, Reb Hirschl might've found his inclination toward its indulgence waning. Drink, by its nature, is an excess that contributes nothing—it only takes away. Reb Hirschl was a man who had reasonably thought that a good few of his problems might be solved in judicious takings-away, but the more time he spent under Anna's leavening influence, the more he came to feel as if a kind of reconstruction might be preferable to the wholesale demolition offered by the perpetually emptying bottle.

However much Reb Hirschl may've benefited from Anna's influence, he certainly didn't benefit any from the Swallow Man's. Perhaps Anna had been naive. She had not assumed that the two men would become the best of friends—in fact, that was one of the reasons Reb Hirschl had so appealed to her—but she had thought that the Swallow Man would, as an extension of herself, take Reb Hirschl on in the way he had done for her, teaching him how to creep through the forest, what plants were good to eat, how to be someone who was not himself—in short, all the ways of the road—but the Swallow Man kept his doors firmly shut to the Jew, and Reb Hirschl remained, despite all her desires, other than "us" in practicality as well as in Road.

More than once, in small instances of—for lack of a better word—neglect from the Swallow Man, Anna had wanted to speak up. "Why," she wanted to say, "why do you not show him the proper way? Why do you leave him outside? Why do you so dislike him?" But to speak against the Swallow Man, to reference the existence of some vault of knowledge or wisdom or benefit in the presence of a person to whom he had explicitly elected not to reveal it—this was undoubtedly a betrayal.

Despite, or perhaps because of, all this, Anna's fondness for Reb Hirschl only grew, and she spent as much of her walking time as she could diverted in his foolish, lovely little world.

Bit by bit the two of them began to shade in their walking song with words. The very first line ("Schlep, schlep, schlep, schlep") came rolling out of Reb Hirschl one day near dusk, and for the next several rounds, he and Anna sang the entire song (with freshly renewed enthusiasm, at the top of their lungs) on this single syllable. In no time they had a full verse.

> *Schlep, schlep, schlep, schlep,*
> *Walking, walking, step by step.*
> *Where we're heading, I don't know,*
> *But schlepping, schlepping, here we go!*

It was nonsense—silliness—but the longer she spent in Reb Hirschl's mind, the more Anna came to understand the earthy wisdom of such foolishness. If you've taken it upon yourself to schlep the heavy weight of the entire world along with you through the fields and forests of Poland, it won't do to sing about it in anything but the lightest terms.

They were in the process of devising a second verse together (what words they had yet to decide upon could always be rendered "schleps") when, in the midst of a wide field of tall wheat at noon one day, Anna made her first contribution to the project. Until now Reb Hirschl had never failed to submit his new lyrics for Anna's approval, and on occasion she might suggest a small improvement, but until the wheat field she had never brought forth anything of her own whole-cloth invention.

"Schlep, schlep, left, right," they sang, "through the day, into the night."

Here Reb Hirschl intended to belt forth several more placeholding "schleps," but hearing Anna beside him, he pulled up short, and she sang her new couplet alone.

> *If we don't know where we're bound,*
> *At least this way we won't be found.*

Anna kept schlepping forward, but Reb Hirschl stopped in his tracks.

"Anna," he said. "That's really good."

She stopped and looked back over her shoulder at him, her eyes narrowing in suspicion. "Don't tease," she said.

"But I'm not," said Reb Hirschl. "That was really good."

Anna stuck out her tongue and ran away.

To the dismay of the Swallow Man, Anna and Reb Hirschl were growing closer and closer, like the two lips of a shoe being pulled in tight by the laces. Some nights, when he thought her asleep, Reb Hirschl would lay his square hand lightly atop Anna's hair and say a little prayer for her. This periodic benediction was the only visible outcropping of what was a more silent tension developing in the space above Anna's head—the prayer was a traditional, formulaic one, intended to be given by parents to children once a week. It was not lost on Reb Hirschl that, rather shamelessly, he did this in the presence of her daddy.

Reb Hirschl had been traveling with Anna and the Swallow Man for some while when she finally began to notice the peculiarity of their travel pattern. In the past she and the Swallow Man had occasionally retraced their steps through the brush, backtracking in the case of an impassible obstacle or a missed opportunity, but ordinarily their routes would never double over themselves. Now, with Reb Hirschl in tow, their path seemed to be describing a loose, looping arc.

Reb Hirschl didn't appear to realize it, but Anna knew that this was not right. It felt idle, like treading water, and what was more, she was afraid that the Swallow Man would lose track of his endangered bird. Anna still kept her eyes open for it whenever she thought to, still desperate for a glimpse, but she had yet to see it.

Anna resolved to find an opportunity to speak to the Swallow Man in private. She had wanted to make Reb Hirschl one of them, but if anything was happening, he was remaining the same and they were becoming more like him, and though she would not articulate the problem publicly, it seemed far too stark to continue ignoring it.

In the end, though, the issue found its own resolution.

The Swallow Man knew of the habitual lightness of Anna's slumber, and so when he spoke that night, it was gently and soft.

"Are you finished?" he said.

Reb Hirschl had just stepped out of his prayer posture, and his concerted devotion fell off of him easily, like dust.

"Yes. I'm done. What, you want to learn some prayers? Usually you're sleeping by the time I—"

"Hirschl. We're going to cross the German lines tomorrow."

"Ah." This cut Reb Hirschl's jollity short before it could even reach its full swing. "So. You've decided to stop walking in circles, then?"

There was a silence, and then the Swallow Man said, "Yes."

"Well," said Reb Hirschl. "That's a blessing. Whole thing seemed strange to me, just walking around and around, but what do I know?"

"The German lines are dangerous to cross under the best of circumstances," said the Swallow Man, "and these, Hirschl . . . these are not the best of circumstances."

"Surely, that is true," said Reb Hirschl sagely. "Surely, you are correct."

For a moment the Swallow Man did not speak, and all there

was was the sound of the night's insects and of the shifting forest. In the distance somewhere, in some far-off settlement, almost beyond the border of audibility, a dog was barking.

"Normally," said the Swallow Man, "if we were going to cross the lines, my daughter and I would pass through a regulated checkpoint, take as little risk and attract as little notice as possible."

Reb Hirschl seemed to take this information in, and then, inhaling sharply through his nose, he lit out in a new direction.

"I've been wondering," he said. "Tell me: What kind of a man never looks over his shoulder when he leads his child into the wilderness? And what kind of a man has food insufficient to feed a single person and still breaks it up into meticulously equal portions when one of the three hungry bellies is his child's?"

The Swallow Man didn't answer.

The stillness of the night was broken by a half-stifled chuckle. "I understand," laughed Reb Hirschl, "you must get hungry. But shouldn't you at least be shorting *me* a bit?"

"Do you recall," said the Swallow Man impassively, "what the condition of your joining us was?"

Reb Hirschl frowned and nodded in good humor. "You told me I was honor-bound to ask you no questions, and I think you will recall that I said I would make no such promise. But don't change the subject. I hesitate to ask, sir, but the man who behaves in this way—is he the kind of man who does not love his daughter?"

Reb Hirschl let this question hang in the air for a moment before he plowed forward. "Well, I suppose this is possible, but then, would such a man suffer so patiently the small, troublesome noises of such a distasteful little fellow as myself only because his daughter has taken a liking to him?

"No. I do not think so. This man, he is not a man who does not love his daughter. He, I think, he is a man who very much loves the young girl . . . whom he *calls* his daughter."

There was another, longer span of empty time now, but this one belonged to the Swallow Man. He remained utterly still, allowing Reb Hirschl's ponderings to float lazily off into the sky. Only when they were completely gone did the Swallow Man speak again, as if the Jew's digression had never even taken place. "It is difficult to pass through a German checkpoint unnoticed—"

"When you travel," said Reb Hirschl, "with *einem Jude?*"

Their conversation had been a gravel pile of German and Yiddish, all intermingled, sliding in one direction and then another unpredictably, but Reb Hirschl picked out these two small, round, smooth words, like pebbles, specifically from the German and held them out to the Swallow Man in the palm of his flat, square hand.

"Yes," said the Swallow Man.

It was so rare an occurrence, Reb Hirschl declining to speak, that it made a serious impression when it happened.

"There is, of course," said the Swallow Man finally, "another possibility. Not far from here there's a gap in the lines. I'm not sure how long it will remain open—the Germans seem to be gathering with some speed—but if we move quickly, there's a small chance we'll be able to make our way through."

"Hm," said Reb Hirschl.

"That is our plan, as of now."

"Ah," said Reb Hirschl.

"Of course," said the Swallow Man, "if we're seen, we will certainly, all three of us, be shot. At the checkpoint, on the other hand—"

"At the checkpoint, on the other hand, only *I* would certainly be shot."

The silence now was an uncertain thing, and for a good deal of time, it remained unclear to whom it would fall to speak next.

"I'm not sure how long you've been traveling," said Reb Hirschl finally, "but up until recently I was in the Lubliner ghetto. I know who gets shot and why, and it's me and for no particular reason."

"Yes," said the Swallow Man.

With a plink and a swish, Reb Hirschl took a drink of the liquor in his small glass bottle and said, "Here. Have some vodka. Would you like some vodka? We can drink together to my imminent demise."

"I want neither to drink nor to see you die, Hirschl," said the Swallow Man. "I just thought you should know—"

"I know. Oh, I know," said Reb Hirschl, and then, "You sure you won't have some vodka? It's never failed me so far."

"That is because the first time it fails you is also the last. I won't give my wits away when the world is like this."

Reb Hirschl chuckled. "Fair enough. You, you're looking for the other side of this whole thing, this war, this world, call it what you will. Me, I'm not sure there is another side. And if this is the world now, well, I want it to have some vodka in it, and some singing. And some fools."

The vodka in the bottle swished and plinked a second time as Reb Hirschl wet his lips. When he spoke again, the tenor of his voice had shifted, and if before he had spoken with polish and sheen—well aware of the humor beneath his words—now he spoke with a dark, warm timbre, unguardedly, as if through his clarinet.

"The girl," he said. "She is very sweet, Mr. No Name. Incredibly good. And you've taught her very well how to survive. I must be honest and say that I am not entirely certain what I think of *you*, but I do not doubt that you are a good man, and if I think so, she is the reason."

The Swallow Man did not speak.

"It's funny—being around her, it almost makes me see you the way she does. That's the difference between being a little girl and being a grown-up: she doesn't realize that you *have* a name, that all of this that you do, it's a protective layer, like she's following around an empty suit of armor."

The Swallow Man was silent. When Reb Hirschl started in again, he had returned to his brassy tone.

"You must be a very interesting man, whoever you are. I would love to hear your stories, you know? Really *talk*."

Reb Hirschl dismissed this fanciful notion with a wave of his broad, flat hand.

"No, I know you're not going to tell me anything, and maybe that's better, maybe that's what makes all of this work, this pretense, but that doesn't stop me from wanting to know. I must be honest, I have absolutely *no idea* who you are underneath there, who the tiny little fellow is, pulling all the strings in that giant puppet suit of armor. The only thing I know is that your Yiddish is far too good.

"But listen. Me? I'm not afraid of being known. Let me tell you a story. Can I tell you a story?"

Now Reb Hirschl breathed in slowly and long through his nose, and held the air for a moment before he spoke.

"A few weeks ago I was in the Lubliner ghetto. We're all there now, the Jews of Lublin, those of us who haven't been moved or otherwise disposed of, and it's squalid and filthy and horrific, and there's not enough food, and Death walks around, daring you to look him in the eye. But! There are still people there, and where there are people, there are gatherings, even if they're illegal. And where there are gatherings, there are sure to be two things: music and liquor.

"This makes me a lucky man, and on two counts. The first: I love music, and I make it well, which means that I am unlikely to go uninvited to many gatherings. The second? I love liquor almost as well as I love music, and when one makes good music, one's cup doesn't stay empty very long.

"I don't even remember why I went outside. Perhaps I was taking a break, or taking a piss, or running an errand, or checking to see if the stars were still up in the sky, but when I walked out through the door, someone pressed this very bottle of vodka into my hand. It wasn't the first time that evening, let me tell you, that my hand had held a bottle, and I stumbled out through that door with my clarinet in this hand and my vodka in this.

"I don't remember whose the gathering was, or if it had a particular purpose, or if it was simply meant to blow a big raspberry in the face of *das Große Reich*, but I remember where it was: I remember that if you turned your head to the left, walking out the front door, you could clearly see the Grodzka Gate. Well, I turned my head to the left, and do you believe it? There was no one there. Not a single guard or soldier. It was open. Simply open.

"I've had a long time to think since then, in the time that you've spent not talking to me. I wonder if I would've gone if I had been sober. I think that I wouldn't have. But I *wasn't* sober. I was piss drunk, and that meant that I realized what I was doing was an invitation to Death only when the thing was half done already.

"I was beneath the arch in the dark when I realized what I was doing. It was my drunkenness that had pushed me to start walking, but I wouldn't be speaking truthfully if I said it hadn't taken a conscious decision on my part for me to continue.

"I said to myself, 'Walk.'

"So many things told me to go back:

"'You'll be shot for sure!'

"'Walk,' I said.

"'But the vodka isn't yours. It's not right to take it.'

"'Walk.'

"'You left your case and all your spare reeds in the apartment! How do you expect—'

" 'Walk!'

"And so I walked. And I left. And somehow I found myself going out from the ghetto, out from the city, and all the way out into the wilderness. Even when the sun rose and I realized that I had no food and no water and that my only reed had cracked, even then I kept walking. I always kept walking.

"Now. Why do I tell you this story? Is it because I think you will understand from it my bravery, or my great self-determination? No. I don't fool myself to think that I am so brave. I was drunk, and I know that men like you are surely braver, even sober, than I am, even drunk.

"Do I maybe tell you this story to convince you that I can pass by Germans unnoticed? No. I am a fool, for certain, but not so great a fool as to think that one absurd stroke of luck may be relied upon for future planning. No, Reb No One, I tell you this story because I want you to understand that I am a man who walks where there is road, no matter where it leads, and where there is no road to be had, I walk through the bush.

"Many men meet their deaths before the appointed time, and do you know why? They stop walking.

"Me, I do not stop walking.

"So, with gratitude for your hospitality—if it may be called that—and for the sharing of your food, I will say this: Whether you point me at a gap in the German lines or you point me at a regulated checkpoint, I will walk. Until I fall."

The Swallow Man was silent. Reb Hirschl took a swig of vodka, and when he spoke again, it was with an airy cheer that would've seemed contrary if it hadn't been so fullhearted.

"So! You have your girl who shouldn't be alive. I have my clarinet that doesn't play. . . . What does she have?"

When Anna woke the next morning, Reb Hirschl was already done praying, and he smiled down at her as she rubbed her eyes open.

"Good morning, *yidele*," he said. "What shall we do today, hm?"

At that moment they were near the ultimate eastern edge of what was called, at the time, the Government General of Poland—the far end of the Wolfish hold on Polish territory—and in order to pass across the German lines and make their way into the Bear's holdings, it was necessary for them to cross the Bug River.

The Swallow Man had chosen a crossing for them with trees close in on either bank. If they made it through the relatively calm water without being noticed, they wouldn't have much ground to cover on the other side before they were out of sight again. In topographic terms the crossing was nearly ideal: the water flowing slowly if strongly, the river not as wide as in other places, and trees to provide cover on either bank.

The only problem was the bridge.

Downriver of their crossing there was a bridge of considerable tactical significance. On the western end of the bridge, the Germans had garrisoned a small detachment of infantry and light field artillery, and during their wanderings the three of them had discovered other groups of armor and infantry support gathered a ways back in the trees. On the Soviet side they could see evidence of perhaps a platoon of riflemen on guard, though there could well have been more.

The plan was to cross as far upstream of the bridge as they could get before they came into the rocky, wider section of the river, where the water became choppy and frothed up. There was some discussion of venturing yet farther upstream and crossing where the current and undertow were a bit stronger—this would keep them out of view of the bridge—but this notion was ultimately rejected, for Anna's sake. Should something happen to the Swallow Man and Reb Hirschl, she might still be able to make the opposite bank, where the water was calmer, but certainly not in the rapids. At the chosen crossing the distance from the bridge was not small, and it was judged sufficient for caution's sake.

No one was entirely sure of the depth of the river at this particular place, but it was decided that they should try, at least, to ford their way through. By now Anna was much taller than she'd been when first they left Kraków, but it was still doubtful that she'd be able to walk the whole way, and the Swallow Man promised to hold tightly to her hand. He was prepared to lift her, should it become necessary. Reb Hirschl offered to carry Anna on his shoulders the whole way, but she thought that this would attract undue attention, and the Swallow Man agreed, adding that it would make her an easy target should any particular soldier decide to begin shooting, and the suggestion was immediately dropped.

It was resolved that they should make the crossing at dusk,

when the sun had sunk beneath the horizon. The growing dark might help them to escape detection, and they might also still gain the benefit of some last dying daylight with which to navigate the forest when they reached the far bank.

Reb Hirschl's nerves were visibly excited by their transgression, and standing beneath the last of the trees before the river as the sun sank into the leaves and branches on the opposite bank, he hopped lightly from one foot to the other.

"So?" he said. "Shall we go?"

"Not," said the Swallow Man, "until you fasten your boots."

Reb Hirschl was very hesitant to do this, and argued, postulating slightly variant iterations of the same fantasy in which he forgot or dropped or otherwise lost his clarinet without its bootlace shoulder strap, but the Swallow Man categorically refused to set a single foot forward until Reb Hirschl's boots were done up.

He spoke in a cold, slightly sharp, and terribly rational voice. "What should happen if your boot should lodge amongst the rocks on the river bottom, Hirschl? Or if you should simply lose it in the undertow while lifting your foot to step? What if a Russian soldier should spot us and we should be required to run once we reach the opposite bank? What if—"

"All right," said Reb Hirschl. "All right. You've made your point," and he began dismantling his clarinet sling in order to lace his boots up.

"At least," he said, "we are crossing from the German side to the Russian. There are fewer of them there to chase us, and

I can't imagine that the Germans will come after us across the bridge."

He pulled his bootlaces tight and smiled up at Anna. "Thank heaven for small mercies."

"Come on," said the Swallow Man. "We're losing our dim."

The Swallow Man had carefully articulated a strict edict before they'd arrived at the river's edge ("Move as quickly as you can without moving quickly. Nothing attracts pursuit so much as flight"), and Reb Hirschl had fully intended to follow this rule when they set forth from the cover of the trees. As it happened, though, Anna and the Swallow Man had thin bodies that cut easily through the water, but Reb Hirschl's broad frame plowed up against it, and he struggled to keep pace with the casual hurry of the other two even at his top speed.

They had nearly reached the opposite bank when the Russian started firing.

It was one at first, a watchman patrolling near the center of the bridge, but it wasn't long before there were five or ten rifles, Russian and German, all firing in their direction. The soldiers shot from where they had been, both midpatrol and from their fortified positions at either end of the bridge, and the bright flashes as they fired speckled the length of the bridge in the dark like tiny stars being born, living, and dying all within a moment.

When people are shooting at you, your gut turns into a black hole. When people are shooting at you, all the blood in your body burns.

Anna's feet caught easily on the riverbank, and she scrambled and pushed herself up against the dry land and ran for the woods. She was halfway gone before she turned back to look at Reb Hirschl and the Swallow Man.

Everything seemed to be happening in the tiny, gasping breaths between bullets.

The Swallow Man had one lanky leg up on the dry riverbank. He was turned back to check on Reb Hirschl. Reb Hirschl was struggling through the river, perhaps two-thirds of the way across. Little patches of water exploded all around him as the bullets missed nearly.

The Swallow Man yelled to Anna, "Make the trees! Go!" and he turned to throw himself back into the river.

It happened just as the Swallow Man had feared it would—Reb Hirschl's fingers failed, and his clarinet floated away from him, downstream toward the bridge, black wood in blackening water. Anna could see it in his eyes: his desire to reach the far bank had been supplanted by the need to retrieve his beloved, foolish, useless clarinet.

Anna was afraid now. She could see how it would happen. When the Swallow Man reached Reb Hirschl and lifted himself from the water, he would not have seen the clarinet float away, and he would take hold of Reb Hirschl and try to pull him toward the forest, and Reb Hirschl would fight him, unwilling to leave the thing, and both of them would be caught and killed and she would be alone.

But the Swallow Man lifted his head from the water and

yelled to Reb Hirschl, "Go! Walk!" and as the Swallow Man disappeared again beneath the water, Anna was surprised to see Reb Hirschl fighting strongly and swiftly, with all his might, through the water toward her.

He had nearly made the bank when the Swallow Man rose from the water only feet from the clarinet. Within seconds he had it, and he dove again, his long body undulating expertly, as if he himself were only a wave of the current.

Reb Hirschl and Anna were at the edge of the trees now, waiting for the Swallow Man, and when he emerged from the water, holding the clarinet like a waterlogged torch, all three of them took off running into the forest with greater swiftness than Anna had ever known at any other time, and then she was running with and for and of her life, and she found herself crying and laughing, whooping with a terrible, indescribable glee at not yet having died.

At the time it seemed to Anna miraculous that they all had passed the river unhurt. It was only that evening, when Reb Hirschl helped to cauterize the wound with one of the matches from the jar, that she learned that the top joint of the Swallow Man's long right pinkie had been shot off.

They must've been pursued, but they saw no Russians that night. Perhaps their commander had judged their force insufficient to lose any men from the defense of the bridge. Perhaps he knew something that the three companions did not know.

As Anna and the Swallow Man settled in to sleep, Reb Hirschl cradled his clarinet in the crook of his arm and prayed with greater vigor and conviction than Anna had thought possible.

That night, or early the next morning, all three of them woke together at the massive, thundering sound of the bombers passing overhead, like all the storms the sky had ever seen playing out at once. Shortly thereafter they felt the ordnance begin to fall on the cities and airfields of Soviet-occupied Poland.

That was the morning of June 22, 1941. Operation Barbarossa had begun. Hitler was invading the Soviet Union.

And they were on the front line.

Operation Barbarossa was the largest military action that there has ever been. Three million German troops and their allies made incursion into Soviet-controlled territory along a front that stretched nearly two thousand miles, from the Black Sea all the way up to the Baltic. The number of bombers that roared over Anna and her companions was so great that the planes seemed to block out the sky entirely.

It was a massive, furious, swift attack.

And Anna thought they were after her and her friends.

They had lain themselves down well away from the road, but as soon as the sun rose, they saw the immense clouds of dust that the advancing German forces had stirred up. It was, of course, only an ill-tended rural dirt road, loosely packed and scarcely ever traveled by anything heavier than a buggy or farmer's cart. When the tires and boots of the mechanized infantry and the treads of the panzer groups began to smash against the road, it reacted the same way everything did—it fled into the air in terror.

The Soviets were shockingly unprepared for the invasion, and most of the fighting that occurred on the banks of the Bug was over long before midday. Anna tried to take comfort, hearing the gunshots fade into the distance, but there is no comfort when the sound that replaces gunfire is the unending march and grind of advancing armies.

That day they stayed precisely where they'd slept the night before, lying quietly on the earth, careful never to stand, nor to move too rapidly. They were far from the road, but who knew where the next column of advancing Germans was to be found, and who knew where the scattered, retreating Soviet defenders might be?

To spend an entire day facedown in the brush is no easy thing. None of the three of them spoke. The noise of the march and their distance from the road almost certainly made it safe to whisper, but none of them seemed to have the desire.

Three times that day, as every day, the Swallow Man took his pills, and three times that day Reb Hirschl muttered his prayers.

It was not until well after dark that the cacophony of the German advance faded into the distance (though for days afterward Anna swore she could hear it just at the very edge of her awareness), and they remained still on the ground for nearly an hour thereafter, until the Swallow Man finally got to his feet and immediately, silently, led them farther into the forest.

There was nearly as much adrenaline in all their veins as

there was blood, and almost no opportunity for disagreement or the release of tension was passed by untaken between the two men, but very likely the original trigger was food. None of them had eaten in the last day at the very least, and the Swallow Man seemed to have no intention of stopping to forage.

The argument reached a head close to the old Soviet camp. It was, of course, not truly old—it couldn't have been deserted earlier than fifteen or twenty hours previous, and there were still fires burning where the bombs had fallen. Over the crackle of the blazes, a record that had been playing during the attack was left skipping, repeating itself over and over, looping two string-orchestra chords endlessly. All the same, the place had a feeling to it of true antiquity—like some ancient temple, doomed to be burned forever and ever in perpetual fire.

The thrust of the argument was this: The Swallow Man felt certain that pursuing the advancing Germans was the safest course of action—as long as they could stay away from the conflict proper, they would surely be the least of the concerns of those soldiers fighting for their lives. Reb Hirschl, on the other hand, thought that moving back across the Bug and retreating from the battle lines was the best option. There could be nothing to help them survive here, no food stores that would go unraided by the vast swarm of Germans that they had seen pass. And besides, since when did the military consist of one unbroken line of attack? Wouldn't there be reinforcements, a second wave, support troops? How could they be assured of staying safely ahead of the next wave?

"How?" argued the Swallow Man. "By not turning around and heading directly for it."

Reb Hirschl shook his head and muttered to himself, "It is not good to stay living amidst death. It is not good to stay amidst death."

Anna was surprised by the virulence of Reb Hirschl's argument—he had, up to this point, never been bashful about sharing his views and ideas, but neither had he ever pushed them when presented with the Swallow Man's authority. Reb Hirschl must've been badly shaken by the crossing, the bombings, the advances, because the argument was long fought, and for a time she doubted if either man would yield.

Finally the Swallow Man spoke, as always when in extremis, with quiet articulacy and decorousness. "Hirschl," he said. "No one will tell me where to go. If you will follow me, then follow me, and if you will go, then go, but I have not slept since the onslaught began, and I have no more words to give you."

Anna was still awake that night when Reb Hirschl finished his prayers, and the Swallow Man tossed and turned uncharacteristically, finding no sleep, either. The fires were burning quieter now, but still, in the distance, there were gunshots and explosions, and throughout it all the record played its two chords, over and over and over again.

The sounds in the world kept Anna awake, but Reb Hirschl had never shown any difficulty in finding rest, and she thought that the Jew had long since fallen asleep when finally, grumbling to himself, he pushed up to his feet.

"Where are you going?" asked the Swallow Man from behind closed eyes. Anna was surprised to find him awake; he spoke out of utter stillness.

"I'm going to turn off that record, is where I'm going," said Reb Hirschl. "For God's sake, at least we could hear a different chord."

The Swallow Man sighed. "I am relatively certain that there's no one left alive in that building, Hirschl, but if there's anyone else even within earshot, and the record were suddenly to go silent . . ."

Reb Hirschl sat back down, hard.

It was only a few minutes before he began singing with the record, lifting and flicking his nimble voice around and between and over the two chords, now fighting them, now embracing them, now turning them about. It was a good thing and beautiful, his singing, but somehow it made Anna extraordinarily melancholy.

His singing lasted near twenty minutes, and then he rolled over onto his side.

The Swallow Man waited until Anna's little tiny snore reached up and joined the Jew's—like a nighttime parody of that obnoxious walking tune—before he rose and walked off into the forest.

In the morning Anna was the first to wake.

The Swallow Man was sleeping just where he'd first lain down. Next to Reb Hirschl, attached to his beloved clarinet, there was a fine leather shoulder strap bedecked with hand-tooled Slavic iconography. It was a thing of beauty.

When she saw this, something fell into place inside of Anna. Ever since the onslaught of the Germans had begun, even by the side of Reb Hirschl, she had managed to forget completely that there had ever been such a thing as gladness. But here in front of her was indisputable evidence that the world was not everywhere on fire, and was, in fact, growing kinder in places—the Swallow Man had ventured out to forage not for food, not for gain, not for his benefit or for Anna's, but only for the surprise and delight of her beautiful Reb Hirschl.

Reb Hirschl was right. It is not good to live your life amidst the deaths of others. Here there were no foolish riddles, no little tunes to sing. Here they could not play at running from one another for amusement. Here they were running in earnest.

The Swallow Man quickly became a carrion crow in that place, and they followed after him in the wake of battle, fleeing before the unseen next wave of death, with perfect trust into places that even he did not know and had never been. None of the three knew that area—Belarus, perhaps, or Ukraine—and despite their penchant for crossings-over, it somehow deepened the distress they felt, being in that place of war. Poland, they believed, they knew. Poland, they believed, was theirs. The border may have been only a line in the sand, but the difference between wandering in your own yard and wandering in your neighbor's feels vast when you are afraid.

Cruelly, of all the time they spent wandering, this was when the three of them ate easiest and most. It was blitzkrieg: the

Germans were advancing as quick and as hard as they could. They left no one—neither the retreating Soviets nor their own troops—the time to stop and pick over the dead, and there was hardly a fallen man that didn't have some small ration in his pocket or pack.

The Soviet rations were those they came to know best— most often cracked wheat or hardtack, but frequently there were sunflower seeds, which they ate endlessly as they walked, collecting the shells in a small bag to avoid leaving a trail. Canned beets were also common, or tins of mysterious meat, sometimes labeled with words that the Swallow Man read out as pork, chicken, or beef, though those labels could best be relied on to say what was *not* in the cans. These rations were so plentiful that Reb Hirschl even had the luxury of declining to consume those labeled pork, though he knew very well that he was likely enough frequently eating it under other names.

German rations were less commonly found, but more likely to contain some wonderful surprise: usually a small fruit-flavored candy or two, and once a bar of chocolate.

Anna's third of the chocolate disappeared almost instantly, and as they walked the rest of the day, Reb Hirschl's dwindled smaller and smaller as he handed her little bites.

"Better you should have it," he said.

Anna never saw the Swallow Man eat any of his chocolate. It was possible that he was keeping it to trade, but he had already stocked up on so much tea for that purpose that she couldn't imagine why he wouldn't simply eat the delicious stuff.

At first Reb Hirschl was terribly hesitant about the prospect of taking from the dead for his own benefit. He did not argue as he had before, but grumbled endlessly, and hardly ever took part in the harvest. When he did, it was only under duress, and if one listened closely, he could be heard in quiet prayer whenever he came into contact with the dead.

Anna quickly became acquainted with the locations and the depths of the various pockets and pouches standard in a Soviet or German uniform, and her small hands learned to work into them with ease. Her only difficulty was in undoing the tight buckles or laces or fastenings that kept things closed, and as the carrion days continued, a system developed whereby the Swallow Man would swoop forward over the dead bodies and undo all their fastenings with his swift, nimble, long, strong fingers, and Anna would follow behind and strip them of all their benefit.

On occasion she would discover some small item of particular use to one of her companions, and she would hide it away for an opportune moment. Once she found a pair of fine leather gloves from a German officer with hands shaped like the Swallow Man's, the right pinkie joint of which she filled with a thin strip of rolled bandage. Anna gave them to him when Reb Hirschl went off into the trees to relieve himself. She said nothing and he said nothing back, but he rewarded her with a smile—rarer, even, than normal in those days—and from that day forward, it was uncommon for the gloves not to be either on his hands or hanging from his belt.

Once, in the pocket of a Soviet officer's greatcoat, she found a glass flask of vodka wrapped in cloth, and she gave it to

Reb Hirschl when the Swallow Man had gone ahead to survey a road he wished to cross. To the Swallow Man it was necessary to give in silence, and without celebration, but when she gave the vodka to Reb Hirschl, she grinned and said, "Better you should have it," and for a day and a half he wouldn't stop singing her praises.

It was not pleasant to harvest from the dead—particularly the recently dead, whose warmth thwarted Anna's efforts at stoicism—but soon she learned not to look at their faces, and if she interacted with only their clothing and their kits, she didn't have to wonder about what their names had been, or what it had sounded like when they sang.

Reb Hirschl, on the other hand, seemed to actively keep himself from ignoring these questions. When he finally began to join the harvest, he quickly made it a policy to look the dead men straight in their faces, and before he launched into his rapid Hebrew prayer, he would greet them politely.

"Hello, sir," he would say, and when he was finished, "Thank you," or, "Please pardon me," or, most ridiculously, "Be well."

He never said so, but it was not difficult to see that the Swallow Man found this an absurd, weak practice.

Once, Anna asked Reb Hirschl what he was saying when he searched the bodies of the dead.

"It's a prayer, *yidele*," he said, "called El Malei Rachamim. It asks God to enfold the souls of the dead beneath the wings of His holy presence and to lift them up like brilliant lights to the sky."

Anna imagined bombs falling in reverse, their fiery explosions contained in swirling spheres of human proportion, flying back up out of the pine forests and into the night sky. Anna could not tell if she thought the beauty of this idea was related to its terror.

"If you'd like, I can teach it to you," said Reb Hirschl. "Or if you just want something to say, you can always just use '*Baruch atah, Adonai, mechaye hameytim.*'"

The Swallow Man sighed loudly, and not wishing to be thought a fool, Anna never said Reb Hirschl's little phrase. But she never forgot it, either.

It was a delicate and peculiar thing, the relationship between Reb Hirschl and the Swallow Man. They did not like each other particularly, would never have called one another a friend or even have associated under different circumstances, and wherever they were, an argument seemed to lie only a few seconds' journey from them in any given direction.

But something had begun to grow between them as well—a sort of cooperative understanding—and the moments in which this was most obvious were the moments in which one of the two men would forgo his own strongly held way of being and embrace the other's, as if giving a moment of his life to his opposite in tribute. For example: Reb Hirschl never thanked the Swallow Man for his clarinet's shoulder strap. Anna was worried, that first morning, that this was an affront or perhaps an oversight, but she quickly saw that this was not the case. It was visibly difficult for Reb Hirschl not to explode with gratitude, and his forbearance in the face of the Swallow Man's habitual, cultivated composure was the ultimate show of thanks. There was no mistaking the contact their eyes made before they set off that morning.

It was perhaps more difficult for the Swallow Man to reciprocate these moments of deference—his ways were so strongly regimented and surely determined, his categories so black and so white—but he showed his affection by slackening in the furious stricture of his sense of order. The time was made for prayer, without reservation or trouble, and comments or little hummed melodies that before would've drawn scorn or an increase in the pace of the Swallow Man's gait were now more easily (if never very enthusiastically) tolerated.

It was blitzkrieg, and the three of them stayed close behind the German advance without much direct threat for two, perhaps two and a half months before the danger began to mount again. This is, of course, not to say that their travels in those days were ever at all comfortable. There was scarcely a day without flame or without the evidence of death at their feet, and it seemed somehow that, almost as a policy, the wild, maniacal blast of ordnance shook the air and lit the sky just when Anna lay down to sleep—as if it knew.

There was not much sleep for her to take in those months anyway.

They had wandered deep into the Soviet Union when they began to feel the threat of counteroffensives against the German advance. They'd stayed far enough behind the line that they hadn't felt terribly endangered by the fighting until this point, but the leaves were beginning to change, and the rain was falling steadily, and the Germans had been forced nearly to a halt. The Swallow Man was afraid to slow too much, lest a second wave of Germans should catch them up, but if they kept at their pace, they would almost certainly meet the back of the first wave.

Not infrequently now they could hear serious tank fire far too close to them for comfort. Reb Hirschl endlessly speculated about the pain of being hit by a tank shell, and while this was hardly the deciding factor in the Swallow Man's determination to turn back to Poland, it could scarcely have bolstered what little resolve he had left.

Together they filled a fallen soldier's pack with as many field rations as they could gather for the return, and with surprisingly little complaint, Reb Hirschl carried the huge, heavy thing all the way back.

At first Anna thought the return homeward simply arduous, and much time was lost lying still on the forest floor while supply vans and troop transports rumbled by on nearby roads. Of course they never traveled on the roads themselves, but aiming to escape the front as rapidly as possible, they couldn't avoid them as thoroughly as they would've liked, either—their traffic was a more reliable indicator of direction relative to the front than any compass or more objective instrument could possibly have been.

It felt oddly relieving, going back toward Poland, as if the entire way were sloped slightly downhill, and they managed to reach the Bug with little incident. Once, caught nearly by surprise, Anna and the Swallow Man had fallen to the ground and held their breath, playing dead for the benefit of a squad of German scouts, who tsked their tongues and lamented the early demise of such a beautiful, obviously Aryan little girl, while Reb Hirschl cowered quietly in a treetop above them, hugging the food tightly to his chest.

When they were long gone, and Anna and the Swallow Man had risen from the fallen leaves on the forest floor, she asked him what the word "Aryan" meant, and the Swallow Man told her that it was Wolfish for "Wolfish." At first Anna felt affronted to have been described in such a manner, but the Swallow Man raised his eyebrows and told her that they were right. She looked very much like a Wolf cub when she slept. This was perhaps the most frightening thing Anna had heard since the war began.

What started arduously ended horrifically.

In their own quiet ways, each of the three of them had begun to feel its presence, begun to understand more and more with every passing footfall, but soon they knew for certain: Death had come to dwell in that part of the world.

She could not now recall precisely when it had happened, whether it had been in the year and a half before they acquired Reb Hirschl, or if perhaps he had been by her side when she'd seen it, but on some wintery day, in some wintery clearing, Anna remembered coming upon a huge dump of old and broken things. They seemed to have been removed from an office building, or perhaps a government ministry, and they had been carefully sorted into piles: here a high stack of chairs with broken legs or arms, there a rank of file cabinets to which the keys had been lost, or the drawers of which had irreparably jammed. In the clearing's center there had been a high mound of broken typewriters.

There had been a light dusting of snow on the ground, but none had accumulated on the discarded things, and boot prints, still wet, had recently sunk into the ground. There was no knowing if or when people might return, and there was no great benefit to be found in filing cabinets anyhow. They hadn't stayed long, but the image of the dump had stuck strongly in Anna's mind.

It was all she could think of when they first came upon one of the mass graves. Perhaps it was the angle of the light, or perhaps that the snow was similarly powdery and sparse, but more than likely what made her think of the discarded office equipment was the peculiar blend of organization and chaos that reigned there.

The edges of the pit were straight, the hole in the ground meticulously squared despite the frozen-earth, but the bodies had flopped in at attitudes that seemed inhuman—feet draped backward toward the backs of heads, arms bent at unnatural angles, faces buried in the bodies of strangers.

This was more death than Anna had ever seen in one place, and its presence here did not feel the same as the small, lingering wake that she'd come to know in harvesting from fallen soldiers. Here the death did not seem to dissipate. Here it felt as if Death were at home.

Anna was uncertain. This was, without doubt, a particular

horror, but despite her uncertainty, Anna acted, and she did what she'd become accustomed to doing. She went to harvest amongst the dead.

This is a rare and unforgettable thing: the texture of a footfall on the chest of a dead man resting on top of others twenty deep—the slight give and rebound beneath the pressure of your boot.

The crows began jealously to cede their meal as Anna advanced to the middle of the grave, and by the time she reached it, nearly all of them had shifted to the trees above to stare down at her, as much with their beaks as with their eyes.

It was not long before the Swallow Man spoke.

"Anna," he said. In all their life together, it was the first time he had called her by that secret name in front of anyone else. "No."

It was not a scolding or an angry no. It was as gentle as anything he'd ever said to her, and when Anna came off of the pile, he placed his long hand tenderly on the back of her head, and it was the closest thing to an embrace he'd ever given her. "I think we shall leave them what they have."

Anna couldn't bring herself to tell him that each of the pockets she had encountered had already been emptied.

"May we please," said Reb Hirschl, standing still at the tree line where they had come into the clearing, "leave this place?"

One of the things Anna loved about Reb Hirschl was the way his singing inflected his speaking voice. No matter whether loud and wry or soft and tender, there was a way of light and brightness in almost every word he spoke.

Almost. Not all. Those six words—"May we please leave this place?"—sounded as if they had been spoken by a different man: an old man, and impossibly tired. They were as dark as closed eyes at midnight, those words, with not a spot of brightness in them.

Reb Hirschl did not speak again for two days, and that evening he did not pray before he lay down to sleep.

They walked back into Poland across the very same bridge from which they'd been fired at when first they crossed the Bug. It was, of course, a risk, and one that the Swallow Man would never have allowed before he met Reb Hirschl, but there was no one in sight, and it gave them all some small sense of pride to do it, as if their passing boot marks could conquer the bridge, sanctify it against all the destruction that surrounded it. Despite their having been within her borders for some time at that point, only when their feet landed on the other bank did they finally feel as if they were back in Poland.

But Poland had changed while they were gone, and she was more like the lands of war and death across the river than they wanted to believe.

# What'll You Give Me?

They kept to the woods in those days. The trees seemed to make the Swallow Man more comfortable, and their trunks and boughs helped to conceal their presence when the three of them needed to disappear.

There is less to say about this period in their wanderings than any other. This is because they took pains that nothing at all notable should happen. Before, Anna and the Swallow Man might have sought out conversation with an affable stranger if the opportunity had arisen, but now other people were avoided at any cost. Even when they discovered the manna of a soldier lying dead amongst the trees, they would pass by his provisions in silence if there was even the slightest evidence of people remaining nearby.

Anywhere, behind the cunning disguise of any pair of mundane, commonplace eyes, Death himself might be found to lurk.

They passed two winters without stopping, as Anna and the Swallow Man had before. Eating became difficult, and each of them lost weight. The Swallow Man, naturally thin to begin with, grew willowy and gaunt, and Reb Hirschl's wide rib cage slowly bared itself of any covering, until the individual bones began to show through his skin when he washed.

Anna would not have tolerated the advantage of an inequitable division of food, had she known. She never felt full or satisfied, of course—none of them did—but somehow her nutrition remained sufficient for her continued growth and development, and by the time they met the Peddler, Anna was beginning to resemble a young woman, albeit a thin one.

Of course, outward changes do not occur without internal ones.

The Swallow Man was a master of easy metamorphoses and Reb Hirschl of secret understandings, and yet between the two of them, they had worse than no knowledge of the intimate mysteries of femininity. The best they could do for Anna was to be where she expected them to be when she wanted them, and to be elsewhere when she did not.

Things were happening to her body—things that made her self-conscious—and where, as a younger girl, she'd felt little shame in simply squatting to relieve herself, she began to require more privacy as time went by.

It was high summer when the Peddler came toward her through the trees, and she had not encountered another living person that was not the Swallow Man or Reb Hirschl in so long that she was immediately frightened.

Of course, in those days it was far from uncommon to en-counter persons who were *not* living. They weren't as numer-ous as the trees of the forest, but over time they came in Anna's mind to be just as natural an outgrowth of it, and by now, whether or not she knew the words, she had memorized the rise and fall and the rhythm of each sentence in Reb Hirschl's El Malei Rachamim prayer. These days he would not continue on his way until each fallen man or woman or child had received the benefit of its recitation.

Anna was squatting in the brush when the Peddler came walking through the trees, and she hurried to stand and cover herself before he noticed, but his eyes found her while she was still completing the process.

This did not help to ease her anxiety.

Another one of the Swallow Man's rules: *Transitions are pe-riods of weakness.* If the choice was between being seen doing something and being seen attempting not to be seen doing it, the former was always the stronger choice. This was true ir-respective of what, particularly, it was that you shouldn't have been doing.

The Peddler's eyes twinkled in a very unsettling way when he saw Anna, though she couldn't say if they unsettled her for their similarity to or for their difference from the Swallow Man's.

"Ah. Hello there, madam," he said in rough, thick Polish.

Oh, he frightened her.

On his back was a soldier's pack very much like the one Reb Hirschl carried, only to this one myriad little bags and boxes and parcels had been strapped or tied, with rope or twine or leather. Despite the warmth, he was wearing a good, heavy overcoat, which hung open to reveal, at first count, three pistols of varying design, and these amongst other weapons. There was a long blade, like a cross between a hunting knife and a short sword, that Anna recognized as a German bayonet tucked into the leather bandolier around his waist, but his pack was of Soviet issue, and his coat seemed to be of civilian orientation. He himself was small, his pack nearly as large as he, and despite his belly and nascent double chin, his frame seemed as if it ought to have belonged to a skinny man.

Nothing about this fellow made sense.

"Hello," Anna replied, doing her best not to sound frightened. She tried to speak as loudly as she could in order that the Swallow Man or Reb Hirschl might hear and come to investigate, but as much as she wanted to lift her voice, it came out tremulous and soft.

The Peddler began to step slowly closer in to her. "You're not out here alone, are you?" He was smiling, but it did nothing to settle Anna's nerves. "It's a long way to the next town, and the woods can be dangerous."

"No," said Anna affably. "No, my friends are just over that rise."

The Peddler stopped just outside of arm's reach and began to lower his pack. "Is that so." It wasn't a question.

Anna smiled as brightly as she could. "Yes, of course. Reb Hirschl!" she called.

She knew that the Swallow Man would almost certainly

have been a more effective defender to her. But she didn't call for him. She called for Reb Hirschl. "Hirschl" was, after all, the only name they had amongst the three of them.

It was, nonetheless, the Swallow Man who came over the ridge first.

"Hirschl, hm?" said the Peddler, casting his eyes up and down the Swallow Man. "I'm not sure I would've pegged you for a Jew. I was just preparing to show your friend here my wares. I have plenty of things to trade, if you're interested."

Before the Swallow Man could say anything, Reb Hirschl came charging over the ridge.

"Ah!" said the Peddler. "*Two* Jews! Young lady has a taste for the forbidden, hm? Unless she's a Jewess, too?"

Anna didn't know how to answer this question. In fact, it was one that she had never considered. Reb Hirschl called her *yidele*, "little Jew," but she had only ever thought of it as an endearment, and no one in her life had ever told her that she belonged—or didn't—to any particular tribe or nation, one way or another.

"No," said the Swallow Man. "No, unfortunately, she is Polish."

The Peddler smiled. "I don't know why you say 'unfortunately.' These days it's hardly good fortune to be running around Jewish. But you probably know that yourself, Mr. Hirschl, hiding in the forest like this.

"Perhaps I have something in my pack that can help you survive your misfortune, hm? Matches, ammunition, food . . . I accept zlotys, reichsmarks, even rubles if you have them, but I

do my primary business in trade. I may even have some chocolate, if there's something special you can do for me. Surely, we
can reach some mutually beneficial arrangement."

It was, at base, an offer of assistance, but from his lips it did
not sound friendly.

Reb Hirschl was about to speak, but the Swallow Man held
up his hand to stop him.

"You've been in the cities?" he said.

The Peddler sighed. "If you're looking for a specific friend
or relative, I'm afraid it's unlikely I'll be able to help you, but if
you'd like to send a letter or a message, I'll see what I can do
about helping it along. For a price."

"No," said the Swallow Man. "All I want is news."

The Peddler smiled his broad, empty smile. "News. News
isn't free. Make a deal with me and I'll tell you what's happening in the world. Though you may be sorry you asked."

They still had quite a bit of the tea that they'd collected during Barbarossa, having neither encountered many people since
then, nor frequently allowed the risk of a fire to do something
as foolish as heat water. The Peddler stuck his nose in one of
the sachets, breathed in deeply, and then nodded.

"What can I give you in return? You look as if you could
use some food. A little cheese? Hard bread? I even have"—and
here he pulled back the paper wrapping of a parcel of middling
size—"meat."

Meat was tempting. They'd run through their stores long
ago, and it was energy-rich stuff, filling and tasty. The paper of
the Peddler's package was open only a brief moment, but what

was inside looked good to Anna—a leg of something, lean and red, still on the bone. There was even some pale hide on it. It must've been fresh.

"What sort of meat is it?" asked Reb Hirschl, and with startling speed the Peddler snatched back the paper, his strong fingers working sharp and furious.

"What the fuck do you care what kind of meat it is? You should be counting yourself lucky to get your teeth into some one last time before you're killed, you fucking cow. Stop asking stupid questions."

For the first time the boiling cruelty that simmered low inside the Peddler had slipped up to the surface, and all three of them took silent note.

The Swallow Man smoothed things over, forgoing the meat and instead selecting some dry bread and a small piece of old fruit. It was late afternoon when they all sat down together, and it was far from their custom to eat at such a time of day, but neither Reb Hirschl nor Anna was interested in questioning the Swallow Man's decision.

The Peddler did most of the talking, while quickly consuming the majority of the food that the Swallow Man laid out, including almost all of the bread they had just acquired from him.

The news was unbelievably horrific. Anna could scarcely understand the things he was saying. By this time the ghetto liquidations were occurring and the camps were operating with increasing efficiency, and the Peddler told stories not only of what he'd seen, but of what he'd heard.

At first Anna thought he was making it all up, afflicting them with the deranged imaginings of his sick mind, but she'd seen more than one mass grave, and when he spoke of it all, he seemed far too stoic to be inventing it for his own absent enjoyment.

Reb Hirschl took the greatest interest in what was going on, which didn't surprise Anna much. Aside from news of the war on international fronts, much of what the Peddler had to talk about concerned the Jews—the increasing stricture of the laws passed against them, the things that were done to them in the streets, and finally, what he'd heard and seen of the camps. Despite Reb Hirschl's questions and comments as the primary conversation partner, though, the Peddler's eyes rarely rested on the Jew. Instead his gaze lingered mostly on the hem of Anna's too-short, outgrown dress. But in moments when he thought he could steal a glance without its being noticed, Anna saw him flick his eyes up and down, back and forth across the Swallow Man's face.

By the time the sun began to set, the Peddler had exhausted his store of news and was leaning back against a tree trunk, idly chewing on some cheese that he'd made no offer of sharing. The conversation had run out of fuel several minutes before, and it seemed clear that soon either he or the three companions would have to leave and go find another camp if they didn't wish to spend the night together. The Swallow Man was stirring, perhaps to make his excuses and set them on their way, when the Peddler spoke again.

"No, no," he finally said to the Swallow Man. "I know you."

This fear had been growing in Anna's stomach all day. She still very much remembered what the Swallow Man had told her on their first day together—what it meant to be found.

"No," said the Swallow Man, not looking at the Peddler. "I don't think you do."

"But your name isn't Hirschl. Is it."

The Swallow Man shrugged and turned his head to Reb Hirschl. "Is my name not Hirschl?"

Reb Hirschl didn't answer.

The Peddler sat forward from his tree trunk. "You're a very peculiar-looking fellow. Your face is very distinctive. Have you ever been to Łódź? Or maybe to Berlin?"

"Łódź?" said the Swallow Man. "Once or twice. Perhaps you saw me there when I visited."

The Peddler was silent for a long moment, and then he said, "Yes. Perhaps."

After another long moment he pushed himself to his feet and began pulling his pack up onto his shoulders. "I may have been mistaken. No matter."

But his voice was not as malleable as the Swallow Man's, and it did not sound like no matter.

When all his straps were in place, all his buckles buckled and his boots laced tight, he turned away to face the gathering dark out in the trees. "Well," he said. "I'm off."

But he did not leave.

It was another few moments before he finally said it. "What if I were to take your little girl here for a short walk with me?

Just for the pleasure of her company, you understand. You know my inventory—you might choose what you like. Or, even better, Mr. Hirschl—I have all sorts of money. What do you think?"

"Thank you," said the Swallow Man, as placid as ever. "No."

Anna knew perfectly well that the Swallow Man would never send her out into the trees with a stranger, but she couldn't help but eye the weaponry that the Peddler had on display. Firearms aside, the blade of his bayonet was almost three times the length of the Swallow Man's hidden pocketknife.

"Are you sure?" said the Peddler. "It's been so long since I had any company."

Anna could not for the life of her understand this. Had they not just sat together and talked with him for three hours?

"And you know," said the Peddler. "Young trees give such sweet fruit. The first fruits are the very sweetest of them all." Then he laughed, high and shrill and startling. "Don't you Jews have some sort of festival? A holiday for the first fruits?"

Reb Hirschl spit on the ground and muttered in Hebrew.

The Swallow Man remained calm. "I'm afraid," he said, "that there is simply no way."

"Ah, well," said the Peddler with small regret, and he turned to go.

Over his shoulder they heard him yell through the trees as he went: "Be careful now, greedy! Too much of that sweet fruit and you'll get sick!"

\* \* \*

They (or, more accurately, the Peddler) had already eaten through the allotment made for their evening meal, and with nothing left for them to do, they settled in to rest.

Anna could immediately tell that both of her companions were ill at ease. Reb Hirschl paced slowly and muttered, and there was a faraway look in the Swallow Man's eyes as he sat sharpening the blade of his pocketknife.

Finally Reb Hirschl spoke up.

"Shouldn't we go? Find somewhere else to be for the night?"

The Swallow Man frowned. "No."

"But he knows where we are. She'll be frightened all night if—"

Anna was already frightened.

"Hirschl," said the Swallow Man, rising abruptly, as if a decision had been made. "I'm going to take a walk. Will you do me a favor and stay with her?"

Reb Hirschl looked like he was going to object.

"It's all right," said the Swallow Man. "Say your prayers. I'll be back."

He left his bag and umbrella behind and walked off into the trees.

Reb Hirschl did not know what to say, so he busied himself with prayer, but even when he'd finished, Anna hadn't been able to find sleep, despite her best efforts. Her belly was painfully empty, and she was anxious.

Of course that night of all nights, the forest was quiet and still. If she wasn't to sleep, Anna longed for some small sound out of the darkness that she might be able to interpret in favor of safety and assurance.

But it did not come.

A great time passed and the Swallow Man did not return.

Reb Hirschl didn't know what to say to her. It was all right that he didn't know. Anna didn't know what to do, either, but quietly she kept wishing Reb Hirschl would sing.

He didn't.

Anna was dozing when the Swallow Man's light footsteps finally approached from the woods, growing softly up into audibility.

She kept her eyes closed and tried in earnest to take her sleep back. Perhaps she did not want to know what had happened. Perhaps she already knew.

The Swallow Man did not speak when he returned. The first words were spoken by Reb Hirschl. "Where did you get this?"

Here Anna cracked her eyes open and saw the Swallow Man carefully adding cans of food to Reb Hirschl's pack. In his hands the Jew held a bottle of vodka.

For a moment the Swallow Man remained silent, and then he said, "There was no point in leaving it."

Reb Hirschl dropped the bottle onto the ground, where it landed with a heavy thunk. "No," he said quietly to himself. "No, no, no, no."

"It was swift," said the Swallow Man. "I waited until he slept. There was very little pain. He barely knew."

"And this makes it right?"

The Swallow Man sighed. "Hirschl, you heard what he said. He could've come back for her at any time. And his weapons were stronger than mine."

"So we get up and we walk her away from here! We don't . . . we don't . . ."

The Swallow Man frowned to himself and hefted an unmarked can. Despite Reb Hirschl's agitation, still he spoke softly, thoughtfully. "No," he said. "No, a man like that hunts. If he wants a thing, he finds it. Running, hiding—that's too little, too late."

"And what . . . what if he'd given up the thought of her? *Then* what have you done?"

"There were other considerations."

"What other considerations? That you didn't like him? He was a hard man, yes, a bad man, of course—I can't even imagine the kind of things he must've done to lay his hands on a leg of meat like that, but—"

"That wasn't a leg," said the Swallow Man, not looking up from his business. "It was an arm."

Reb Hirschl sputtered, laid his fingers to his lips, and turned his head away. After a long moment he began to shake his head. "No," he said. "No, I don't care. Even if that's true, we've run up across far too many men as bad as or worse than he for it to make a difference. The only reason you killed this one and not any of the others is that he knew you. You were scared."

The Swallow Man stopped packing away what he had brought back and turned to Reb Hirschl.

"It's true," said Reb Hirschl. "Isn't it?"

"It's not a question," said the Swallow Man slowly, carefully, "of how bad he was, Hirschl. He was *dangerous*. What makes you think that a man like that would even hesitate a moment to say where I am if he thought it would benefit him?"

"What?" Reb Hirschl was genuinely shocked. "I don't care who you are, and I don't care who knows it! This thinking, this . . . You've become one of *them*! You're a spiller of blood, a . . . a taker of life! And *why*? To keep your name hidden?"

"Suffice it to say, Hirschl," said the Swallow Man, "there are things about me that you don't know. It is imperative that they not find me, because if they do, they will take me, and if they have me, the entire *world* will become a taker of life, as you put it.

"Listen to me very carefully, Hirschl: The world itself. The sky will burn.

"Are you so narcissistic that you think the simple slaughter of one man of such low quality as he is an unreasonable price to pay for the prevention of that possibility?"

Reb Hirschl could not stop shaking his head. "I don't know what you're talking about, whoever you are. What I know is that *life* is what matters. Life is the only important thing. The world is filled now with men who have decided that they know who should die and who should live for the Betterment of Everything, and I had thought that you were numbered amongst those of us who cared enough to protect the holiness that is just a single living, breathing person."

"I will not be an instrument of death," said the Swallow Man, and this pronouncement seemed more final than any Anna had ever heard before. "That is why I keep my secret name safe. At any cost, Hirschl. Any."

"To keep yourself from becoming an instrument of death, you kill?"

"Yes," said the Swallow Man. "Yes." And then, almost as an afterthought, "Each man is the steward of his own soul."

"Yes," said Reb Hirschl, "yes, yes, yes, you are your own steward, and though it may sicken me to have walked beside an extinguisher of life, I have no authority over you to tell you what you may or may not do. That authority is God's alone."

Reb Hirschl took a moment to calm himself, but when he began to speak again, though his voice was softer, the tension of it was just as great, and despite his effort, his volume grew and grew again in agitation.

"I first came with you because you offered me sustenance when I had none of my own. You, whoever you are, you are an intelligent man, maybe even brilliant—surely you must know that I stayed with you only for fear of what might happen to that tender, kind, good-hearted girl who follows after you. I thought I was protecting her from the darkness out there in the world, but maybe the danger was walking beside me the whole time.

"How can you dare to justify yourself this way when her name is written beneath yours in the Book of Life and Death? The name that you stole away from her? How can you possibly teach her to take her sustenance from the bodies of the dead when you turn and make more corpses with your own hand? Certainly, whoever you are: kill to your heart's content if you are only your own man. Lord knows how many others there are like you, so go ahead, do it, be one more. But if you would dare to make this girl, this girl whom you so delight in instructing, who breathes only when she has seen how you do it first, if you would make her like *you* are, then you are *worse* than a killer, you are a *maker* of killers, and I will keep her from you at any cost."

At this the Swallow Man stood up swiftly to his full, towering height. Despite Anna's growth, the Swallow Man continued to loom over her, and now he stood far above Reb Hirschl, too. The Jew seemed so youthful and flush to her, and the willowy Swallow Man so ancient and weary, but when he spoke, the Swallow Man spoke with iron authority.

"Hirschl," he said. "If you try to take the girl from me, I will kill you."

It was true. He did not raise his voice—he so rarely did, and never in anger—but there was something in the measured tone of this simple sentence that felt incontrovertibly truthful, more reliable than anything he had ever said to Anna before in any language.

Reb Hirschl cast about for some way to respond to this, and his eyes caught on Anna's. She was curled up on the ground in a sleeping posture, but her eyes were wide open, and by this point she made no attempt to hide the fact that she was watching the two men fight.

First he saw her, and then he recognized that she had been following their entire conversation. His jaw tightened, and he looked to the Swallow Man and then back to Anna.

There was a question in his eyes. An expectation.

Perhaps she was caught off guard and did not really understand that Reb Hirschl wanted her to speak in his support.

Perhaps he was overestimating her precociousness, and it simply wasn't in her to enter with impunity into such an argument of conflicting morals.

Perhaps there was a fear in her that if she allied herself with Reb Hirschl, she would take upon herself the Swallow Man's threat.

Perhaps she was frightened and could not find the words to say in time.

Or perhaps, very simply, she was the Swallow Man's daughter.

Anna did not speak.

Reb Hirschl made a little joyless chuckle in his throat, and turning away, he walked out into the dark forest.

The Swallow Man sat down hard and sighed. He lifted the new bottle of vodka to his lips.

It was nearly a week later that they found Reb Hirschl's body.


It is not good to stay living amidst death.

This is true of the deaths that drop bodies in rooms and streets and forests, but also of the deaths that linger behind our ears and gummed up at the corners of our eyelids, like settled dust on our clothing, or even like dirt beneath our fingernails— the deaths that we carry along with us.

It is not good to stay living amidst death.

But attempting to think of that time—of those days in that place—without an understanding of horror is like trying to draw the spaces between fingers without an understanding of the fingers themselves.

All the same, I will spare you the details of what happened to Reb Hirschl.

When Anna and the Swallow Man came upon his body hanging from a tree, they cut it down, and sat him up, his back against the trunk.

Anna did not speak.

The Swallow Man, too, was silent. It cannot have helped that what they'd used in place of a noose was the fine leather shoulder strap that he had found for Reb Hirschl and his clarinet.

The clarinet itself was nowhere to be seen.

There seemed to be no words worthy of speech, there and then, in any of the myriad languages between Anna and the Swallow Man. A word is a tiny moment of time devoted to the conjuring aloud of some small corner of what is—"apple," say, or "running"; even "fully" or "mystery." But there was no significance to anything that was, in that moment, only what was not.

And so they stood in front of Reb Hirschl's body in silence. Anna cried. The Swallow Man did not embrace her.

She wished there were something that she might do for Reb Hirschl, some final favor that she might give, as if to button up his coat and brush off his shoulders before he went on his way, and this was all the more important to her because she had so horribly failed to give him what he'd wanted, what he'd needed, the night that he departed from their company.

She tried to imagine what Reb Hirschl would have asked for, but no illumination visited her mind. It had never been difficult to discern what had delighted this poor, sweet man in life—he had not guarded his pleasure in any way—but what he had *wanted* was more obscure. He could never have been seriously praised as an undemanding man; his very existence had taken significant stores of energy to witness. But it was a surprise for Anna to realize that she could not recall, in a single instance, one request that he had made for his own benefit.

When Anna asked herself what he would have *done* for himself, though, all her uncertainty evaporated.

If she had paid attention, she might've remembered the words of the prayer, but Anna had heard Reb Hirschl recite it so often that, despite her lack of effort, the cadence and music of each line, its rise and fall and rhythm, were simple enough for her to reproduce. For words she simply babbled. Gibberish.

The Swallow Man had heard the prayer, too, just as often as she, and as soon as he realized what Anna was doing, in glorious, foolish deference to feebleness, and to indulgence, and to irrationality, he joined in with her.

Instead of nonsense words, though, he reproduced the melody of Reb Hirschl's prayer for the dead in the language of the birds.

When the prayer had finished, Anna cast her eyes upward, and there was a tiny moment in which she thought Reb Hirschl's end upon the tree had somehow enchanted it. Despite the high-summer season, the canopy above them was lit up with colors—yellow and white and orange and green and iridescent blue and red and brown and even black—and then one of them turned its head, and this motion fractured the magic into a hundred little pieces of sky.

The birds were haphazardly arrayed in the branches of the tree, crowded in wherever they could fit, but there was a surpassing decorum to their still gaze that very much made Anna want to begin crying again.

The Swallow Man had never been one in the particular habit of acknowledging surprise, but then he gave a little intake of breath and said, "I—I had not thought that so many would come."

He put his lips together and called as he had done all those many, many lifetimes ago in Kraków, and sure enough, a bright-blue-and-orange swallow flitted down to his finger. Gingerly the Swallow Man lifted the lapel of Reb Hirschl's jacket and nestled the bird inside the breast pocket, close to his stilled chest.

"He'll stay there," said the Swallow Man, as if to Anna. "He'll protect Reb Hirschl—keep the crows off. He'll be all right." And then again, "He'll be all right."

Anna's mind conjured, suddenly, an image of a far-off time when there would be nothing left of Reb Hirschl but a bearded skeleton, a time when the swallow would build himself a nest inside the broad ribs of the Jew's chest.

They left that place and walked the better part of an hour before Anna turned them around. When they returned to the body, she swiftly found what she was looking for. To leave Reb Hirschl's last reed, cracked though it may have been, to eternity with a corpse—even his—would've been a betrayal of what Reb Hirschl had lived for. She took it from his loose, sagging sock and tucked it into her own.

Anna did her best to ignore the fact that every single bird—even the sentinel swallow that had been left in his jacket pocket—had departed.

Walking is a constant. No matter what the pace or the gait, first one foot falls and then the other. To certain people this is a kind of comfort, but it is an undeniable fact that the drumbeat of two pairs of feet falling on the face of the earth makes up an impoverished repertoire of rhythms in comparison with the drumbeat of three.

The Swallow Man had been stoic as long as Anna had known him, but there had always been a liveliness behind his eyes, a sort of gleam that had shepherded her through even the quietest periods of their partnership. Now whenever she had the opportunity to look into those eyes, she found them cold and tired and empty of resolve, like two vacant lots whose buildings have long since been forgotten.

In quiet and in isolation Anna and the Swallow Man saw the autumn come.

The Swallow Man finished the bottle of vodka that he'd taken from the Peddler, and left it empty in the woods.

The autumn began to pass.

They did not talk quite so much anymore, and when they did, their speech was mostly utilitarian in its purpose. There were no more stories, no more tales or lessons or explanations of things in the terms of the road.

Anna had not understood that the Swallow Man had cared so much for Reb Hirschl. Perhaps neither had he.

The number of tablets left in the Swallow Man's brown bottle began to dwindle lower and lower, and now whenever he would take one of his thrice-daily pills, Anna became accustomed to hearing the Swallow Man recite the short formula that Reb Hirschl had taught her as an alternative to his prayer for the dead.

*Baruch atah, Adonai, mechaye hameytim*—"Blessed are you, my Lord, who puts life in the dead."

It is perhaps no surprise that this formula was pronounced, three times a day, with a bitter edge.

As winter approached, the number of pills left in the Swallow Man's reserves fell so low that the tablets rattled in the bottle with every step he took. Anna was sure that any day now they would make one of their rare stops in a city. She wondered whether she would be allowed to cross in from the wild this time, or if, like the last time, she would be left out in the trees.

But neither of these things occurred. The pills simply ran out, and almost immediately the Swallow Man became something terrifying.


The Swallow Man was not an easy person to be around if you were not assured of his friendship. There was a sort of simmering threat that seemed to live behind his eyes, and if he was not a man whom you knew how to trust, then the quiet confidence, the fierce poise, the collection, the sense of waiting and anticipation in his resting muscles—whatever it was that made him the Swallow Man and not simply a tall stranger, that could be a terror.

That thing was the very first part of him to go. He became nervous, and the quiet assurance around which his entire being seemed to have been constructed turned quickly into a writhing column of anxiety. Suddenly Anna was traveling with a stranger.

Winter had come. The previous two, they had not settled in the way they had done before, but now they were without Reb Hirschl again, and Anna couldn't imagine passing another winter on the move without her old Swallow Man to help. And he was hardly the same person. He began retracing routes, sometimes pacing up and down the center of a valley over and over, back and forth again, for an entire day.

He stopped sharpening his knife.

He sweat profusely despite the extreme cold.

His hands began to shake.

There had always been an unspoken trust between the two of them, Anna and the Swallow Man, and she had rarely felt compelled to speak to him directly of practical issues, but now he seemed to be making decisions almost completely at random, and when she spoke up to ask about their plans, he grew irritable and said scathing, hurtful things to her in his smooth, placid voice. Later he would demonstrate no memory of this having ever occurred.

Eventually she had to stop asking.

When he walked (which was now every moment that he was awake, even pacing in circles around Anna as she fell asleep), he rubbed his hands together or twisted the long fingers of one hand around the knuckles of the other.

If she needed to, Anna could pretend to herself that he was not losing weight, not growing even thinner, that his skeleton wasn't beginning to show through his papery, sallow skin, even despite his increased appetite. If she needed to, Anna could simply stop herself from thinking about it. But when his hair began to break off, she knew that things were not going to go back to normal on their own.

Soon he began to babble, saying all sorts of odd, disconnected things, things that she couldn't grasp even when she understood which language he was speaking. It took far too long for Anna to finally realize that it was not a fault of hers that she couldn't understand him, that the things he was saying were, at best, small fragments of sense scattered so randomly and so thick as to drown out all semblance of their meaning, and eventually, exhausted by the futility of it, she gave up trying to talk to him at all.

In those days he almost always walked so quickly that she was unable to keep up, and the day she stopped trying to communicate with him, Anna asked her question to his back, off in the middle distance, more loudly than he would ever have thought prudent had he been himself.

The question itself was not particularly notable—some invented curiosity, some meaningless inquiry after their course—

and bare days later she would not be able to remember what she had asked.

But this was not the important thing. The important thing was the Swallow Man's response.

He didn't break stride, didn't pause or turn his head or even increase his speed. He just kept walking steadily. Walking away from her.

Never before had the Swallow Man failed to come up with an answer for a question of Anna's, no matter how unsatisfying it might've been to her.

That particular moment—its sensation of the unavoidable knowledge that the Swallow Man was beyond her reach—was the loneliest and most isolated time Anna had ever known in a short life that had been long on solitude.

Something was clearly happening—clearly *had* happened—and it was not difficult to see that the something was dangerous. Of course it hurt Anna not to be the Swallow Man's immediate intimate anymore, but aside from all that, and aside, even, from the terrifying, gigantic question of his health, things clearly could not continue the way they were going if she intended for either of them to survive for very long.

The *dwór* was only supposed to be a stopgap at first. It was an entirely unsuitable situation—the nearby village was too small and too close, and furthermore, everyone there was acquainted. It had been nearly impossible for Anna to walk through the streets without feeling as if those she passed knew she shouldn't be there. Under any other circumstances at all, she would have passed by the *dwór* at some distance, but at the time she needed to feel as if she were in control of what was happening, and even if it was false, a closed arena for a few hours would at least give her the *illusion* of some control. If she had feelings of guilt at the thought of caging her Swallow Man, well, they were easily mitigated by his increasingly feral, unpredictable ways.

Besides—it was just so beautiful.

A *dwór* is a Polish manor, a seat of the nobility built on a country estate, and this one was as old and as grand and as huge as any. The ceilings were carven, figured wood, and the windows were green glass, and its halls and rooms spread out, rambling, it seemed to Anna, unendingly in every direction, back and out from the great portico at the house's center.

She thrilled the moment she saw that porch, with its tall, strong columns. They immediately reminded her of the palace that stood behind King Solomon in her book of illustrated children's tales back in Kraków, and Anna felt somehow that if she could make that *dwór* the place where she belonged, if she could find a way to stand in front of it the way that Solomon stood in front of his palace, it would make her safe and prosperous and great—as if simply belonging there might cure the Swallow Man.

Perhaps it was not belonging *there* specifically that Anna so deeply, so almost spiritually wanted, but simply to belong *somewhere*.

It was the largest single house she had ever seen. City girl that she was, Anna thought at first that it must be some big, old country apartment building, but the moment they were inside, the Swallow Man identified it.

"Ah," he said in Russian to no one in particular, "a place to make people think they're better than others," and he spit on the floor.

It was clear that the *dwór* had been used by the Germans at some point as a kind of regional command center or bureaucratic field office, but they mustn't have been there long, because the house seemed frozen in transition.

In one bedroom lush curtains framed the windows, fine upholstery adorned the furnishings, and the shade of the linens on the meticulously made grand old canopy bed had been carefully selected to cohere with the color palette outlined in the rich wallpapering. Everything, beneath the layer of dust, was arranged just so, to a degree that Anna had never before seen.

Directly across the hall, though, a room that had been designed with precisely the same level of painstaking care was rendered a riot: mismatched furniture from every corner of the house—wingback armchairs, plain wooden three-legged stools, a candy-striped satin settee, a gardener's bench, even a heavy gray velveteen sofa—all crowded around a long, wide dining table that had been shoehorned into the room, forcing the bed back awkwardly against the wall. There was a regional map tacked crooked against the fine wallpaper. Cigarette butts littered the floor, and papers, mugs, and empty ration tins were everywhere.

It was as if two places were attempting to occupy the same house at one time: the first an ornate seat of the gentry, and the other an industrial military command.

It was difficult to know who to be in that house.

At the beginning Anna worried that perhaps they might round a bend in some corridor and encounter a pack of German soldiers. Then, once it had become clear that they had all gone, she worried that they might return at any moment. Soon enough, though, she passed through a doorway and saw the reason they had left: as huge as the house still was, a third of its expanse had been demolished by a bomb or a shell or some other sort of explosive, and it all lay where it had fallen in a huge pile of rubble.

Perhaps it was truly three places trying to occupy the house, then: the elegant country manor, the military command post, and the battered, chaotic shrine of destruction.

Anna chose simply to ignore the cold, blue, frozen hand at the end of the uniformed arm that rose up from the rubble. Better simply to stay away from the destroyed third of the house. Best not to look it in the eye.

At first Anna harbored the hope that they might happen upon some richly stocked neglected pantry, but whatever food there had been in the *dwór* had long since been eaten or packed away by retreating soldiers, or else by other scavengers like them. Anna's belly complained endlessly of hunger. The Swallow Man's mind was beyond practical considerations now, and she knew that if she didn't find them something to eat, no one would. And soon there would be nothing left of either of them to be hungry.

Anna never thought of the Swallow Man starving. It seemed impossible in her mind for him to die in the same ordinary way that other men did, but it was a very real fear to her that he might continue to get skinnier and skinnier, until one day his clothing would simply fall empty on the ground and he would be gone.

The problem was that she couldn't just instruct him to stay in one place. No matter what Anna did, the Swallow Man would wander and pace and roam, and it was only by her continual efforts that he remained within the house itself. She was terrified that if she left to go after food in the town, his wandering might lead him out, away from the *dwór* and away from her. Worse yet, even, to where people might find him, and who could say what the end of that might be?

Finally, though, the answer presented itself.

Two days now Anna had spent lying on her back, trying to convince herself that she was not as hungry as she was. Following the Swallow Man vaguely around the *dwór* was her only respite from this activity, and he had his own ineffable wandering inclinations, which she found more exhausting than distracting. He might stand in one place, examining some facet of the wood for a full hour, or for ages he might meticulously walk the grid formed by the tiling on the kitchen floor, back and forth and back and forth across the room. Even when he was simply haunting the hallways, she couldn't be assured that he wouldn't, without explanation, break and run off full speed down some corridor. After a while, as long as she had a close enough watch on him to know that he was still inside the house, she was content not to hover over him. Once every couple of hours, she would seek him out, following the noises that all old wooden houses make when even the lightest feet press against their floorboards, until she found him talking to himself in the chapel, or running his fingers carefully over each individual sconce in the downstairs passage.

One day, though, Anna woke from the sort of daytime sleep that can never quite prevail against the gnawing hunger in your belly, and she couldn't find the sound of his feet anywhere. Her first panicked thought was that he must have wandered away from the house, but there were no footprints in the snow, and even he couldn't walk as lightly as that. She scoured the *dwór*, but the only sign of him that she came upon was the pair of fine leather gloves that she had given him in Belarus, tossed into a brimming washbasin, the rolled-up bandage waterlogged at the end of the right pinkie.

In the house's eastern wing, on an upper floor, there was a door of dark wood that had managed to remain shut and locked despite all the tumult the *dwór* had gone through. Time and time again, Anna had seen the Swallow Man walk up to it, lay his hand lightly on its impassive knob, and, finding it immobile, pass on to other quarters of the house. It was in front of this locked door that she found him that day, sitting on his knees, his head pulled down low so that he might face the lock at eye level. Just when she came down the corridor, he managed to trip the locking mechanism with the tip of his pocketknife, and the bolt slid back with a thunk.

The Swallow Man crowed with glee.

It was a library—a gentleman's study appointed in dark wood and lined with hundreds of calfskin-bound books—and from the moment the Swallow Man stepped inside, he never showed any sort of inclination to leave.

They had been sleeping in the kitchen at the very bottom of the house—the large stove had a great supply of chopped firewood stacked by its side, and the warmth of the fire had always been enough to coax the Swallow Man down. But that night he never came, and so it simply became Anna's duty to carry the wood up the long staircase from the kitchen to the small fireplace in the library at the top of the house.

The truth is that it was more comfortable sleeping there. Though the fireplace was smaller, the room was as well, and where, in the kitchen, she might've been woken suddenly in the night by a draft of air, in the library she was never too cold to sleep. The fireplace was set deep in its own little fortified nook, and the single window was covered with a heavy brown curtain, which left the study dim no matter the time of day or night.

Though he remained in motion, the Swallow Man never once made any move to leave his new nest throughout that first day, and Anna told herself that if he passed a second one within the study of his own volition, it would be safe to leave him there on the third and go out seeking food.

The problem was that by the end of the first day, she would

gladly have gone another week without eating in order to avoid having to spend even a moment longer in the study with him. At least when he had had space to roam, the Swallow Man's psychoses had remained, for the most part, inside of himself. She had been able to deal with what little overflowed the bounds of his mind, blocking out most of what he muttered as long as she wasn't required to be too close to him, but now that he had found his nest, the Swallow Man began slowly to transfigure it into a diorama of his bleeding mind, and Anna could bear neither to watch him do it nor to avoid its observation.

It was a slow process. The very first thing he did was to carefully unpack his bag. Things of importance, such as his fine clothes and his identity documents, he threw unceremoniously into the corner. Things like the battered tin drinking cup, his glasses case, his whetstone: these took places of special prominence, carefully laid out like offerings on an altar, on the writing table that he had drawn up in front of the door.

The large black umbrella he opened and secured by its tip to the small chandelier that hung from the ceiling, as if, at any time, the ceiling might begin to drop rain upon him.

And then he started in on the books.

All of them.

In a furious tempest of activity, he threw them from their places on the shelves down into chaotic piles on the ground, and then each successive volume was lifted, and both sides of each page were swiftly but intensively examined. This procedure was occasionally performed with the book upside down.

Most of the volumes were abandoned unharmed, but some—those that met with his immediate disdain—were violently hurled into the fireplace.

Those leaves, though, that particularly pleased him (and these seemed to have nothing notable in common) were carefully cut from their bindings, and soon a pattern of pages grew, laid out in concentric, semicircular ranks, like rays out of the sun, emanating from the fireplace.

At entirely unpredictable intervals the Swallow Man would interrupt this work with a start, consult the immobile face of his broken pocket watch, and dash to his bag.

At first Anna could not see what he was doing, but this behavior repeated itself quite frequently, and despite her fright, she could not help angling for a better view.

It was a tiny little thing that she had never seen before—a little shoe, too small for anyone but an infant, covered in minuscule, bright beads of pink and white and gold, which, one at a time, the Swallow Man pulled off and swallowed with a full cup of water.

Anna did not have to hear what he was whispering to know the words.

*Baruch atah, Adonai, mechaye hameytim.*

Perhaps the most disturbing part of his nesting ritual was the moment in which, with great care and with awful ceremony, he used his whetstone to shatter his hand mirror. This he had mounted on the back of the library door, and he often stared into it for long periods of still, uninterrupted time, which would terminate unexpectedly in a great flurry of motion, and he would throw himself back into the books.

Once a mirror is shattered, there is no knitting it back together again.

Now whatever causeway of communication there had been between the two of them was not just vacant—it was obstructed, dammed, blockaded at his end, and if ever Anna spoke to him during all this work, she was met with the hysterical reprimand "Not now, Greta!"

Anna hadn't the faintest idea who Greta was.

All of this was unsettling, to be sure, even very frightening, but what finally put Anna over the edge was the singing.

There had been a time when she had fullheartedly embraced the idea that she and the Swallow Man were two partnered conservationists, that they were following the last example of a rare and beautiful bird around a battleground upon which an endless pack of Wolves and a Great Bear the size of a continent were pitched in endless war. The Swallow Man was a wonderfully compelling storyteller, and she was very thirsty for stories, but something in the Peddler's slaughter or in the death of Reb Hirschl had shown her the truth hidden beneath the story hidden beneath the truth of the world.

Anna could no longer say with honesty that she felt sure that a soldier from Germany was not simply a soldier from Germany.

This is not to say that in any way she had ceased to think of the Germans as Wolves or the Soviets as a Great Bear—just, perhaps, that she learned late the way in which the rest of the world understands stories, not as absolute, irrevocably factual truths that simply don't exist, but as flaccid allegories or metaphors.

Either way, by the time they'd taken up their place in the *dwór*, Anna no longer believed these things the way that she had when first she heard them.

Until the Swallow Man began to sing.

It was not a certainty. In fact, perhaps that is how her fear is best understood: it was a grave uncertainty.

This man whom she loved, who was certainly responsible for her current existence in the world, who had quietly and placidly and without complaint or second thought provided for her under the most dire and extreme circumstances, this man:

He was losing his hair.

He was wasting away.

His mind, it seemed, was becoming less and less human with each passing minute.

And now, every so often, he would cock his head to the side, there in his nest of madness, and sing to himself, little giggling calls and chirrups and twittering songs in the language of birds.

How was she to know? How could she be confident that he himself was not slowly becoming a bird? Or, rather, that he was not slowly returning to his natural form? That he would not one morning spread his wings and fly away into the sky?

And then how could she track him? Despite his promise, he'd never taught her the signs.

He would be gone.

Anna did not want to think it. Anna wanted to be out of his room.

The night after the first full day in the study, Anna awoke to the sound of shattering glass, and, heart in her mouth, she sat sharply up, but it was not the sound of a great bird escaping through a closed window—it was the sound of a deranged man shattering a small jar that, up until that evening, had held his most valuable possessions: cigarettes and matches.

She watched him—crouched down, maniacal eyes close to his work—in the dim flicker of the dying fire for perhaps ten minutes. He was playing with fire, cutting apart his box of matches bit by bit, burning the striker panel with one of the matchsticks, scraping the residue away with a jagged piece of the thick glass jar. Anna did not know whether to be saddened or frightened at this mad experimentation, and finally she passed into sleep with the exhaustion of holding such tremendous questions tight inside of her.

# Endangered Species

Early in the morning on the second day, Anna left to wander the
*dwór* on her own. There was a moment in which she was afraid
that the Swallow Man might follow her out, but he didn't, and
to her great shame, for a moment she thought of just walking
out of the old house and leaving him there, going off into the
forests and plains and wetlands to fend for herself alone.

But she did not.

That evening Anna returned to the study, where the Swallow Man sat, draped in his overcoat, chittering to himself, a
book raised up on his knees. Nothing in his demeanor indicated that he had noticed her arrival, or even her earlier departure. In the morning, she thought, she would leave again and
go to find food in the town.

But she did not.

Again Anna was woken in the night, but this time the Swallow Man was as well, and, like an animal, he leapt to the defense.

There were voices in the corridors, and heavy footfalls.

The sound was obscure. Who was to say how many they might be? Last night she had been unsure whether to be saddened or frightened when she had awoken. Now there was only one feeling in her: pure, unmitigated terror.

It surprised Anna to realize that she was afraid not of German soldiers, or of incursive Soviets, or even of local Poles; instead, she found that she was afraid of the Peddler, utterly convinced that, open throat or no, he would follow wherever they went. He would find them.

The Swallow Man was on his feet, light and swift, before there was even time for speech. This was the first time Anna had seen the revolver, which he took from the bottom of his bag and tucked into the back of his pants, beneath the hem of his loose, baggy shirt. She did not find its presence reassuring.

In a flash the Swallow Man was out of the study, and Anna hurried to follow, but before she could even reach the door, he turned back to retrieve the great, long coat, which he draped about his narrow frame like a protective mantle of thick-woven dark. His hands fell easily into its deep pockets, and again he darted, light and silent, out into the corridor.

The clomping boots they had heard belonged, luckily enough, only to a pair of local boys. Neither could've been even a handful of years older than Anna herself, but they thought themselves terribly important, terribly adult, in undertaking their quest up to the *dwór* on the hill, and the rough, sharp grain alcohol that had been purloined from beneath an older brother's pillow was, of course, an integral part of this maturity.

Anna heard them talking before she saw them, and the swish of the liquor in the small bottle they passed between them only made her miss Reb Hirschl the more.

"No, idiot, I saw smoke. I promise."

"Are you sure it came from here? There's smoke everywhere nowadays."

"Yes, stupid! It was coming out of one of the chimneys. If someone's in here taking things, my father will want to know. He says if anyone deserves this estate, it's us. Our family has been working this land since before there was even a *dwór* here."

"Fine. But I'm cold. When I'm right and this place is as empty as always, can we just go home?"

Their little boots and little voices drew closer. At any moment, it seemed, they would round the corridor's corner and discover Anna and the mad Swallow Man, and there would be nothing the two of them could do to stop the boys from raising the alarm. But just as the boys passed into view, the Swallow Man tucked her into the small inlet of a doorway behind him and leaned back, half hidden in the corridor's own shadow, against the wall.

The sharp flicker of the boys' overbright lantern served two purposes: it kept their young, round faces very well illuminated, and it kept them blind to the lurking contents of the dark. Without intending to, Anna's mind replayed the Swallow Man's old lesson:

*Carrying light in darkness is an invitation to be snuffed out. Learn to keep your sight in the dark.*

"You ought to be more careful," said the Swallow Man softly, aiming his eyes at a point in space just ahead of the boys, "about claiming things that are not your own."

The bigger boy swore and nearly dropped the small bottle in his fright, but the smaller boy did what small boys always learn to do in times of conflict and war: he lifted his father's pistol and pointed it at the Swallow Man.

The Swallow Man did not flinch. He did not move even the smallest muscle, despite the answering weapon that sat silently pushing its handle into his back. It was as if he were completely unaware that he was under threat at all, or as if he simply didn't care.

It was this second possibility that more concerned Anna.

"It *is*," said the smaller boy. "It *is* mine, this house. My family deserves to have it. And who are *you*, anyway? This place isn't yours. I've never seen you before, and I know all the members of the family that used to live here."

"No," said the Swallow Man, rubbing his palms together smoothly, over and over. "No, I've never lived here before. All places like this belong to me. Empty, half-eaten noble homes, rivers in the moonlight, forests of silence—these places belong to me in a way that they can never belong to the people who only *live* in them. These places are *mine*."

Anna believed him. She was confident that she knew as well as anyone else alive who and what the Swallow Man was—she had been welcomed to live inside his curtain—but still, she believed him when he said these impossible things. Because he was speaking the truth. And it took her heart away.

The larger boy was very clearly shaken. No human sort of thing ought to be able to make the claims that the Swallow Man was making.

"Who?" he said. "Who are you?"

The Swallow Man turned his head away from the pistol and locked his eyes onto the pair blinking out of the chubby boy's face. "You don't know?" he said, and he smiled in a distinctly unfriendly fashion.

The bigger boy, who carried the bottle in one hand and their lantern in the other, took a slow step backward. "Sergiusz," he said. "Sergiusz, it's Boruta."

Anna could not recall anyone at all having first taught her about Boruta—he was of the class of bogeymen that seem to creep, unbidden, into the minds of children. Like all the young of Poland, she knew him very well, and though she was quick to reassure herself that it was not true, that the Swallow Man and Boruta were not the same thing, it seemed an apt fear—perhaps more apt than the boy knew.

Boruta is a demon well known in Polish wisdom and lore, a lurker in marshes and forests, a trickster, tall and thin and dark-eyed, most famous for winning the castle seat of a fourteenth-century king by magicking his carriage up out of the mud. Like most devils, demigods, and demons, Boruta has often been encountered in forms other than his own—sometimes as an old owl or a horned fish, but most often as a huge, black, vast-winged bird.

It was not true. Anna's Swallow Man was clever, and he used stories to clothe and protect himself like armor. This was only one of those stories.

It was not true.

Except in the sense that all of the stories that the Swallow Man told were true, which was a very real sense. Held still behind his back, Anna fought hard against the urge to physically shake the idea of Boruta the Swallow Man from her head.

Sergiusz, whose trembling arm was beginning to tire of holding the pistol out, laughed, just a bit too loudly and just a bit too insistently for the darkness of the hallway. "Of course that's not Boruta. Boruta's only a story."

The Swallow Man said nothing.

"And besides," he said. "Boruta is from Łęczyca, and Łęczyca is hundreds of miles away. Why would he be here?"

The Swallow Man frowned and shrugged, busying himself with the inspection of his fingernails. "Oh, war moves everyone around. You boys haven't known the aftermath of a war yet. You'll see. I've known more wars, beginning and end, than you have little teeth in your little mouths."

The big boy nervously probed at his teeth with the tip of his tongue.

"This is ridiculous," said Sergiusz. "You're just some old hobo Gypsy or something. I'll tell my father about you, and you'll never make it to the end of *this* war."

The Swallow Man had been leaning against the wall, and he stood now, drawing himself up to his full, absurd, spindly height. He did not sound angry when he spoke, and that was, perhaps, the most frightening thing.

"It is unwise," said the Swallow Man, "to speak with such certainty of things that you do not understand."

In standing, he had tucked his hands into the deep pockets of his overcoat, and now he withdrew them with grave deliberateness and began, as before, slowly, smoothly rubbing them together.

"You will find, Sergiusz, that in such circumstances you are not often correct."

The big boy gasped and dropped the lantern, which blinked out quickly. In the sudden darkness it was much easier to see what was happening.

Anna was standing behind the Swallow Man, so the first thing she saw was a faint, pale, flickering glow, dimly illuminating the pallid faces of the boys.

Where he was rubbing his hands together, the Swallow Man's skin had begun to smoke, and then to glow with quiet green fire.

Young boys are impulsive, foolish things. Even when they are fleeing in terror, even when they are frightened and unsure, they fire their fathers' pistols, even if blindly—and even when they are fleeing the great demon Boruta.


Anna wept as she dragged the Swallow Man back to his study, and she was terrified, and she was panicked. For all she knew, she was dragging a demon to safety, but even that was not what so terrified her—for all she knew, she was dragging a demon to safety, and what most frightened her was that she didn't care.

When she had begun to move him, the Swallow Man had been laughing, and by the time she had him back in the library, he was chittering like a bird. She had no idea when the transition between the two had been made.

Anna anticipated a terrible battle in getting him up, getting him out, but even in his madness, the Swallow Man knew as well as she that those boys would not soon forget what had happened to them in the great *dwór* on the hill, and that whether or not they intended to come back themselves, the stories they told would quickly bring others poking about.

Her main struggle was in finding a way for him to walk. He had been hit, struck by at least one bullet in his hip, and he couldn't put any weight on his right leg. His inability did not, however, preclude him from trying, and as Anna dashed around the room collecting as many of the Swallow Man's belongings as she could lay her hands on, over and over he laid his foot softly on the ground, and over and over he muffled a cry of pain.

She was trying to get him to lean on her shoulder, which required him to stoop, when Anna hit upon the solution. The umbrella was sturdy and tall, and if he used it like a cane, he could move at speed with a minimum of pain.

But it was once they got moving that the real troubles began.

It wasn't that he didn't understand the importance of moving quickly—Anna firmly believed that—but she'd lost count of the number of days since he'd ingested anything but beads, and what was more, as they hurried away from the *dwór*, she could see small droplets of blood stretching out in a trail behind them in the snow, like Hansel and Gretel's bread crumbs. He was losing blood quickly, and no matter the strength of their conviction, it could only be a matter of time before he fell, and when he fell, he very well might never get back up.

Every passing step felt like a step toward death, but all the same, Anna knew that they couldn't stop. Even if they found a place to rest, they were still far too close to the *dwór* to be safe, and regardless of whether they were moving or stationary, there was still, despite it all, a trail of blood that would lead any even marginally industrious pursuer directly to them.

There was no reason to keep going, except that to stop would be worse.

Anna was cold, but she walked.

Anna was tired, but she walked.

Anna was hungry, but still she walked, unsure that the Swallow Man could continue without her example. She was as certain then as she'd ever been that she was directly facing her own death. And still—Anna walked. It would have been easier than ever just to lie down in the snow and give up, and after two hours' trek the prospect seemed even more wonderfully seductive.

Anna could feel the emptiness of her own body.

It seemed inevitable. There was nothing left inside of her.

But in the distance, just cresting the horizon, she began to hear and see a small encampment. They were far, far from the battle lines there, but if Anna had had to guess from the way the men were carrying themselves, she would've said they were coming back from the front and not going out to it.

Now Anna had two opposing pieces of information in her head.

The first was something she knew for a certainty from her own experience: as much as they did anything, German soldiers killed people, and she had no strong sense of when they did it or why.

The second was something that the Swallow Man had taught her long ago:

*Human beings are the best hope in the world of other human beings to survive.*

Anna did not know for certain that the tall man tottering over his umbrella by her side was, in fact, a human being, any more than she knew with certainty that a given soldier was a human being and not a rabid, feigning Wolf.

But one thing she did know: there, in that moment, in the dark of that night, she did not like the look of her death. There was no reason—she simply hated the cruelty of the world too much to let it beat her.

And so Anna made a decision.

When they were about a hundred yards out from the camp, its reflected light just beginning to illuminate their approaching silhouettes, she whispered aloud, "Fall over, Swallow Man," and without comment or question, he obliged.

It must've been a field medic or surgeon that stood by the tree, but when she grew close enough to see the bloody splotches that stained his white apron, to see the completely red hands and forearms that lifted his cigarette to his lips, all Anna could remember was what the Swallow Man had taught her:

*Anyone wearing any red at all ought to be avoided. The dukes and captains of Wolves and Bears frequently wear red somewhere on themselves.*

One half of Anna was as certain as anything that someone bedecked in so much red as this Wolf could only be a great sovereign, a great emperor of Wolves. Perhaps oddly, perhaps obviously, it was the half of her that was convinced that the Swallow Man was only a human being and not a demon that held this fear, but by the time she'd recognized the blood, it was too late anyhow—the Wolf had already seen her.

"Please," said Anna in the finest German she could muster. "Please, sir, my father . . ."

The soldier heaved a heavy, put-upon sigh, dragged hard on his cigarette, and followed her out into the snow. It seemed as if it were the most natural thing in the world that a little German girl and her wounded father would come to him for help out of the snow—as if this were the ninth time today it had happened.

He moved with terrible and practiced ease, injecting the Swallow Man with a syrette of morphine, examining the wound, sprinkling some procoagulant or antibacterial powder over the bleeding, binding it up with a gauze bandage. He sounded bored and tired as he lifted his canteen of water to the Swallow Man's lips and spoke.

"He's lost a lot of blood. Hopefully, the bleeding will stop soon, but he really ought to be in bed. Danzig's not far. You should be able to find him a room there. Eventually that bullet will need to come out, but for now just get him to bed."

Many people talk about the sort of desensitization to human suffering that must've been necessary for the Germans to have killed as many as they did during that war, and surely they are correct—dehumanization opened the gates to thousands and millions of evil acts—but Anna and the Swallow Man benefited from the phenomenon that night. In its absence neither of them might have survived.

The soldier was only doing what he'd done a hundred times before—treating the wound and ignoring the man.

It would be easy to dismiss the virtue of his help in this way, to say that he was only acting like a cog in his machine, just like the rest of the German mechanism in those days, simply following his training—except that he stopped halfway to his encampment, and, turning, he jogged back to hand Anna a small, thick, rectangular paper package, inside of which there was a thick chocolate wafer.

He didn't speak.

He didn't smile.

He turned and went back to his camp again.

This time Anna gave the Swallow Man all of the chocolate, and he finished it alone.

\*   \*   \*

It was morning by the time they made Danzig, which is the German name for Gdańsk. The night had been long, and Anna had struggled to make her feet carry her forward. Staring at that German encampment, she had made a decision—to get help not simply so that they might survive until the morning, but so that they two would live. As long as they could. That neither the Swallow Man nor his daughter would die.

Anna never abandoned that conviction up until the very end of her life.

She knew there would be food in Gdańsk, and she knew they could get their hands on it one way or another. If they had to eat scraps and garbage, they would. No one will ever go hungry in a city on the sea if he or she can forget the word "dignity." That was one need taken care of.

Anna also knew there would be medicine somewhere in the city, and that if ever her Swallow Man were to regain himself, he would need that medicine. But she didn't know what kind of medicine would help.

Psychosis and opiates are, however, a potent mix, and with the Swallow Man under the influence of the morphine, any direct inquiry she made earned her not the simple name of a pharmaceutical that she might request from the proper apothecary, but rather an elaborate tale designed to explain that Boruta did not take pills, that instead, three times a day, in order to gain mastery over the secrets of fire, he swallowed the shrunken eggs that were produced in the mating between the phoenix and the *żar-ptak*, the firebird, brought to him by a baron amongst the hummingbirds as tribute for a good turn he had once done them long, long ago. Under any other circumstance Anna would've gladly embraced this story as a thing of filigreed beauty, but all she wanted now was the name of a drug, and by no means would he tell it to her or even admit that he required any.

They found an alleyway in Gdańsk, truly so narrow that it might not even have merited that name. It was a gap between two stone buildings, one red and one gray, and the ground was littered with so much detritus that Anna could hardly imagine anyone had been there before them for decades. No one other than a child or a man as unnaturally spindly as the Swallow Man could have fit into the space.

They ate what, to them, felt like a feast—so much, in fact, that Anna vomited and kept going—though it was hardly the size of a light meal, and all of it harvested from trash heaps and gutters. Anna could scarcely move for the pain in her belly that day, and needless to say, the Swallow Man showed no sign of movement other than his low, steady, animal breath.

When she recovered herself, Anna began to wonder what she might do next. Certainly, they might stay where they were for several days more, recover their strength before moving on again, so long as they made little noise, but there was still the problem of the Swallow Man's medicine. She couldn't understand any way forward without it—not any way that could lead to a place she wanted to go.

So she resolved: she would not leave Gdańsk with any Swallow Man other than the one that had taken her out of Kraków.

She would find him medicine.

It was a desperate plan, entirely harebrained, but at the time it was all that Anna could think of: she would find a pharmacy and she would break in by night and she would look amongst all the medicines, and anything that remotely resembled the small, round white pills she had become accustomed to seeing the Swallow Man take, she would bring back.

This led her, on two counts, to the Swallow Man's bag. First, she needed as much room to carry things inconspicuously as she could muster, and if she emptied the Swallow Man's bag, she could bring back many more bottles than she might if all she had to rely upon was her two hands. More bottles meant more possible successes.

It had also occurred to her that if she was going to wander the city streets after dark with a laden bag, it would not be un-intelligent for her to carry a knife.

When she had tucked it into her waistband (she did not mind taking it from the Swallow Man because she knew that at the small of his back he still had his revolver), Anna set about emptying the bag.

In their hurry to vacate the *dwór*, Anna had failed to recover everything that the Swallow Man had taken out of his bag to begin with. His clothes were there, and his identity documents, and, thank goodness, the knife had been as well, but what re-mained of the cigarette collection was missing, as were the whetstone, the shattered mirror, the tin cup. . . .

The bag was nearly empty when she came upon it—only the

spilled box of ammunition and the baby shoe remained float-
ing at the bottom as it came up in her hand: the small brown
glass bottle, now empty, in which the Swallow Man had kept
his cache of pills.

"Ohhh," said the Swallow Man, giggling like a child. "You
caught me." It was the first thing he'd said since they'd crossed
into Gdańsk, and the third and final time that Anna heard the
Swallow Man laugh.

On the bottle, in a loose German hand, was written, "Potassium iodide, 130 mg, taken orally three times daily, if you want
to keep your wits about you."

If the German surgeon had not helped them, Anna would likely
never have been so emboldened. But then, if the German surgeon had not helped them, they would likely never have made
it to Gdańsk.

It was not hard for Anna to find a pharmacy—there were
several—but she took pains to find the one that seemed best
prosperous, and this was a mistake on her part. Prosperity in
time of war is rarely the mark of the scrupulous.

It was cold and clean and bright inside, and Anna quickly
made another mistake—she spoke German.

"I'm sorry, sir, to bother you—"

"What is it?" His German was not refined, nowhere near
the clipped, educated level of Anna's own. His language was
clearly Polish. She had missed the mark. She had spoken first.

"My father," said Anna. "He's very sick. He needs medicine."

The pharmacist did not seem at all impressed by this, but he did stop what he was doing to turn and face her. He let out a heavy sigh. "What's wrong with him?"

Anna was not sure how to answer this question, so she said, "Potassium iodide. A hundred thirty milligrams. He needs many."

The pharmacist raised his eyebrows. "Potassium iodide! This is not a common thing."

Anna's heart leapt into her throat. If it was uncommon and this finest of the pharmacies in Gdańsk did not have any, could she be sure of finding it anywhere? "Do you have any?"

The pharmacist sighed again and crossed his arms. "I do. But it is expensive."

Anna began, quietly, to panic. She had forgotten all of the Swallow Man's rules. She had spoken first, she had asked for a thing instead of allowing a friend to discover her need, and furthermore, she was now locked into a transactional relationship.

"I—I," she stuttered, "I have no money." It was true.

The pharmacist frowned. "A shame for your father."

Now there was no way back. Now there was no becoming an endearing friend. Now Anna was only herself. Her stomach pinched and squirmed as if it wanted, of its own volition, to flee the pharmacy.

"But, sir," she said. "Sir, he'll die."

"Without potassium iodide?" said the pharmacist. "I doubt it. He might suffer, but I can't imagine he'd die."

"But I don't want him to suffer."

The pharmacist raised his eyebrows again, and after a tight, silent moment, he said, "Come with me."

It was never an offer, never couched in terms of something that she might accept or reject. He simply said, "Come with me."

It happened very quickly, but it felt interminable.

He was a very handsome man, the pharmacist, and it was unlikely that he ever had much trouble getting what he wanted from grown ladies, but in fact, perhaps this lack of trouble contributed; it was the gaining of mastery, the overcoming of trouble—it was the getting of the thing, the Anna—that paid the pharmacist.

His back room was dusty and unswept. The walls were made of coarse red brick, which was nowhere to be seen in the front of his composed shop.

It was exceedingly cold.

There was a chair, old and battered and makeshift, in which he sat, and he put a clear glass bottle—large, full of small, round white tablets—on the floor in front of him.

He never touched her, never rose from his chair, only spoke and instructed, and Anna did what he asked.

He was the first person ever to see her body bare.

She was cold, and she held herself for the sake of warmth, but he instructed her to stand uncovered, and so she did.

He told her to take and hold certain positions so that he might see her display certain portions of her body, and she did what he asked.

He did not touch himself while she was there, and he did

not touch Anna, either, though when he had her facing away from him, she was afraid that he would. He did not threaten, or berate, or bully.

He asked her to do things, and she did them.

You should not misunderstand—Anna was a child, and he was an adult. He held the responsibility. But she was a child who knew how to survive. She was a child who knew that adult-sized animals were not always good, ought not always to be trusted. And she was a child with a knife hooked over the waistband of her skirt.

She took the knife off of her body the same as she did her skirt.

She did the things he asked her to do.

Anna had had no instruction or preparation. She knew that her body had been changing. She knew that there were differences between bodies, and that some men wanted the kind of thing that she had. She knew that it felt powerful and frightening and dark and bright and cold and sharp when they did, in the way that vodka feels warm in your belly while your fingers remain freezing.

He saw her, without any stories to protect her.

He saw her, and for the first time in years, she could not help being Anna.

She cried, of course. Not while it was happening, nor when he rose and told her quietly to take her pills and get out, nor even in the bright light of the front room as he hurried her toward the door, or the white daylight of the street as she struggled to pull the last of her clothing back on, but finally, blocks later, holding the cold glass bottle against her chest, the knife pressing against her hip. She did not cry for long, but she cried.

She quickly came to wish that the thing that had happened in the back room of the pharmacy never had.

But she never came to regret it. She had gotten the potassium iodide.

Anna had expected that the pills would work like magic, that instantaneously, when the first tablet passed the Swallow Man's lips, he would return to her, collected and orderly and tall, the way he had always been.

But that is not the way the world works.

She sat with him in the narrow space between the buildings. It was weeks before he began to return to himself, and that period was the worst in Anna's entire time with him.

They were still.

Though she would not have been able to tell you so at the time, Anna had broken a part of herself like a piggy bank to pay the pharmacist's price, and it felt to her as if she had already failed to uphold her vow: perhaps the Swallow Man was coming back to life, but it felt very much to her like his daughter was dead and buried. The pharmacist had shown her Anna, and she could not find the way back from her.

This is what Anna did not know:

Notwithstanding what she felt, the daughter of the Swallow Man was not dying or dead. In fact, she was hatching, pushing herself up out of her egg, the egg made of shards of porcelain piggy bank, for the very first time.

At least the Swallow Man did not resist his medicine.

Winter was beginning to break when his mind returned. She must've been scampering about the city periodically, collecting scraps for their consumption, but in her mind all that Anna did in those weeks was sit near him where he lay on the ground, and wait, and remember.

It was out of this slow, unending stillness that he spoke.

"Anna," he said. "I'm sorry."

It always surprised Anna, the way that one moment a person could be completely calm, and the next, like a stab wound, like a spasm, she could be crying.

"I missed you," she said.

"I know," said the Swallow Man. "I am sorry."

He began talking again, slowly, over days. Anna's Swallow Man was returning to himself, but now, instead of the monument, the pillar of defiance and brilliant, beautiful deception that he had been, there was a stoop in his height. He could not be what he had been for her before.

She had seen his Anna.


The Swallow Man's convalescence continued. With every passing day he grew stronger, and eventually he began to walk with Anna around the city streets for brief periods. The bullet was still embedded in his hip, and he did not walk with ease, but he quickly regained some fluency in his stride, and if there was pain, he learned to disguise it.

The Swallow Man had made for himself a complex lifestyle of silence, and over time Anna had learned to recognize its different aspects. Now, though, as he recovered his strength, she became acquainted with a new one: he was silent in a furtive, defensive fashion, as if his eyes were always a second away from avoiding hers—as if he was embarrassed at the weakness of having a body prone to injury.

This was no demon.

On one of their walks, he paused, retraced his steps several feet, and turned his head to a certain angle, as if, like a film projector, it were replaying a memory out through his eyes and onto a very particular patch of masonry. "This is Gdańsk," he said. "We're in Gdańsk."

Anna nodded.

"Huh," he said.

It did not take him long.

It rained the next day, and from sunup to sundown, the light remained an hourless, overcast gray beneath its blanket of thick, dark clouds.

They took time and pains to ensure that their fine city clothing looked its very best, and then they walked under the great black umbrella to a dark wooden door in an old building.

The street was cobbled, and the road ran along the slope of a hill. Despite having marched for years through muck and snow and every dirty thing, Anna stood tiptoe in the middle of a paving stone so that the rainwater might pass her by in the thin cracks between the stones. She knew the importance of dry feet.

An older German man opened the heavy door. He was wearing a fine suit that had not been well cared for. He looked back and forth several times between the two of them until, all at once, like a sudden explosion, he realized at whom he was looking.

"My God," he said to the Swallow Man. "I didn't think I'd ever see you again."

The Swallow Man didn't speak.

The German welcomed them swiftly into his house, and as the Swallow Man shook his umbrella dry of rainwater, the other man spoke. "I have to say, I don't think this beard suits you at all."

She hadn't realized it—it had been slow and incremental—but the Swallow Man *had* grown a beard. It was thick now, like Reb Hirschl's had been.

She thought it suited him very well.

The Swallow Man never said that he needed to speak to the older fellow in private—he scarcely said anything at all—but shortly they packed Anna off into a sitting room, and she remained there alone as the two men went into an adjoining space, some smoking room or study, to talk.

A fat lady brought tea and a plate of cookies for Anna and did not speak to her. Anna drank the tea but felt nauseous when she thought of a cookie. She left them on the plate.

She could hear the guarded voices of the Swallow Man and his elder in the next room, seeping out in tiny, supercharged particles through the cracked door.

". . . war effort?"

". . . committee . . . practically stalled . . . well, you know, but . . . still . . . fissile material . . . thermonuclear temperatures . . . tremendous pressure to . . ."

". . . know you think . . . contribution . . . flatter myself . . . something of an asset."

"Yes, of course . . . never thought . . . without you."

". . . few ideas . . . remember, we . . . research into . . . working on enriched . . . supercritical mass . . . chain reaction. Which would . . ."

". . . think . . . weaponized?"

"Yes. I think so, yes."

". . . safe?"

"That . . . can't say."

Abruptly the voices broke off. Anna leapt to look as if she hadn't been straining to hear, but no one came into the sitting room.

There was an old clock somewhere nearby, ticking loudly.

Suddenly Anna heard a sharp intake of breath from beyond the door, and someone spoke.

"Why have you come here, Professor?"

An unseen hand reached out and softly shut the door that had been left ajar between their room and hers, and soon the voices beyond it began to rise in a manner that was not entirely friendly. Anna strained to hear what they said, but she managed to discern only one further word, spiking up beyond the rim of their hush, through the barrier of the heavy wooden door.

"Bargain."

The furnishings in the old man's house were grand, almost as nice as those that had been in the *dwór*, and the presence of so much thick fabric, so much carven and varnished wood, made her uneasy.

There were many beautiful things inside the old German's house, so many possessions and furnishings on which to snag her attention, but what Anna noticed most was the sound of the rain, like a stream of little pebbles against the aged glass casement.

She had forgotten what rain felt like from the indoors.

After one of the longest spans of solitude she had known since she left Kraków, the door to the next room opened again, and the old German followed the Swallow Man out. No one spoke. The Swallow Man held out his hand to Anna, and she went to join him. Whatever strange pleasure the old man had taken in seeing the Swallow Man on his doorstep had gone, and though she did not believe that the two were angry with one another, neither seemed happy when they emerged from the next room, either.

The older man's eyes lingered, almost sadly, on her face.

The Swallow Man was retrieving his umbrella when the older man spoke. "Professor," he said, and the Swallow Man turned, slowly, studiously avoiding Anna's eyes. "If I do this for you . . . if you disappear again . . . they'll come after me, too."

The Swallow Man did not move, but beneath the thick stubble of his unmown cheek, Anna could see his jaw clench once, and then twice again.

"Yes," he said.

None of this was discussed in the days that came. It had never been the Swallow Man's way to explain to Anna what he was doing, the decisions he was making, but she knew as well as he that the dynamic of their relationship had changed. As much as he had been her caretaker, now Anna, for her part, however briefly, had also been his. It felt somehow dishonest to behave as if it were otherwise. And yet they did.

About a week later Anna and the Swallow Man began frequenting certain central points in the city together. At precisely noon on each successive day, they would pass by one of three major landmarks: the Basilica of Saint Mary the first day, the Neptune Fountain the next, the Artus Court on the third, and then back to the basilica again the following day. Every day they would groom their fine clothes in preparation for this outing, and they would take all of their belongings along when they went.

There was never any explanation for this.

It was on the way to one of these outings that the Swallow Man, without turning his head to look at her, said, "When I killed the Peddler, it was with one smooth stroke."

Then he stopped, turned to Anna, and, with the tip of his shortened right pinkie, touched five points around his neck. "Jugular vein, carotid artery, trachea, carotid, jugular."

He began walking again. Anna did not say anything.

"One smooth stroke," said the Swallow Man.

It was at the Neptune Fountain that they finally met the old fisherman.

In his hand he held a small bundle of white cotton.

The Swallow Man seemed delighted to see him, greeting him as an old friend. The fisherman did not speak very much at first, and when he did, it was in an accent that Anna did not recognize.

The Swallow Man passed several minutes engaged in the sort of politesse and personal inquiry that Anna had not heard since she and Professor Łania had gone visiting with their friends of different tongues all those thousands and millions of lifetimes ago in Kraków. The Swallow Man seemed to know the fisherman, and although the old fellow rarely got a word in edgewise, it comforted her to know that he was a close friend of the Swallow Man's.

Shortly the Swallow Man found himself looking at his old copper watch. "Ah!" he said. "Is that the time?"

Anna knew that the watch had long ago stopped ticking, but the fisherman didn't. By now it was second nature to her, living in a world that twisted and squirmed in order to line up properly with fact, and she didn't even give it a second thought.

"You know, my friend," continued the Swallow Man, "I really must fly—I have a pressing engagement, something I simply must attend to on my own—but I would dearly love to hear more about what your life has been, how you've been passing your war, you know, and so on. Why don't you take my Greta out onto the water? I'm sure she'd love it, and I can meet up with you later."

It was hardly the first time the Swallow Man had casually applied a foreign name to her, and she might've been mistaken, but Anna could not recall an instance in which it had sounded so very much like an accident in his voice.

"Ah," said the old fisherman. "This is her."

Anna wanted to ask what he was talking about, but the Swallow Man had turned to Anna, and his fishhook eyes probed into her own, demanding her close attention. "I will meet up with you later," he said. He was looking closer into her eyes than perhaps he ever had before.

It made her uneasy, but Anna knew to trust the Swallow Man. In fact, she knew very little else.

They were about to part when the fisherman spoke to the Swallow Man again. "You remember the bargain? He said you were to give it up to me," he said in choppy, hushed German, and the Swallow Man smiled and said, "Of course."

He did not give the fisherman the small box of ammunition, but he reached into his bag and withdrew the revolver, nearly dwarfing it in his large, long-fingered hand, and with only the slightest hint of hesitation, he passed it to the fisherman.

In return he received the small bundle of cotton.

It was a subtle exchange, and a passerby would not have noticed it, but the Swallow Man knew Anna had, and he smiled at her calmly, unwrapping the cotton and glancing down to verify the contents of the bundle.

For a moment Anna thought he meant to give her the nearly entirely unbeaded baby shoe, but after a tiny, uncertain moment, he closed up the cotton around it again and tucked it swiftly into his pocket.

Then, turning to Anna, he leaned on his tall umbrella and placed one long hand on his hip—his left, at precisely the place where, in the waistband of Anna's skirt, his pocketknife was still secreted away.

"Ah," he said. "You'll have such a good time on the water!"

His voice sounded so bright, so pleased.

"Now, I don't think you shall need to, if you shouldn't want, but remember: if you *should* need to row"—and here he lifted his long-fingered hand nonchalantly from his hip and seemed to wipe some sweat first down one side of his neck and then the other—"the proper technique is with *one smooth stroke.*"

The fisherman chuckled. "No oar," he said. "Engine."

"Ah. Well, then," said the Swallow Man. "As I say, I don't think there shall be any need."

He took the old fisherman's weathered, knobbly hand in his own then and said, "All right! Must fly. I'll meet up with you later."

Without another word he turned and crossed the square. Anna kept her eyes on him as long as she could, just long enough to see him make a slight detour in order to walk through a flock of grounded, resting pigeons and scatter them skyward.

And then he disappeared, around the corner of a building, forever.

# EPILOGUE
## The Uncertainty Principle

There was nothing for Anna to do inside the little rust-red rowboat, no road upon the water with which to keep her feet and mind moving, and so, instead, she worried.

Her eyes could find no distinction between the gray of the sky and the gray of the water. There seemed to be no horizon anywhere, neither behind nor ahead, no thin black strip of land to show where the sky ended and the water began. Anna couldn't help thinking that maybe there was no distinction at all anymore, that perhaps she had slipped into a huge, empty sphere of iron water, over the inner surface of which the old knotted fisherman would pilot her now, forever.

As soon as she had conceived this thought, Anna wished she could forget it.

The sky was thick and gray over the sea, and though she tried, she couldn't determine where the sun had hidden itself. Now and again she could hear the cries of unseen birds, carried out over the open water like the chatter and cackle of ghosts. None of the songs seemed familiar to her.

Time was passing—that she knew—but she couldn't tell how much. Minutes and hours began to feel indistinct, like cups and gallons and teaspoons of loose and lazy water all intermingled beneath the belly of the boat. Forty seconds; forty days; forty years.

Every so often Anna's eyes would, by accident, catch on the old fisherman's, and he would smile kindly, which made everything worse. The only thing that stood out from the gray of the world now—perhaps the only thing left *in* the gray world—was that old man in his bright yellow slicker. And he was not the Swallow Man.

That, of course, was her greatest worry. There had been a time in her traveling, and not so long ago, either, when there wouldn't have been a question in her mind—no matter where she washed up, the Swallow Man would be there, too.

She could not in good conscience convince herself of this any longer.

This was not the whole of the trouble, though—much more difficult to accept was the idea that, still, he might find his way back to her. Disappointment, though heavy, is an easy enough thing to pack away in a suitcase—it has straight edges and rounded corners, and it always fits into the last remaining empty space. Hope is much the same. But somehow the hybrid of the two is something much less uniform—awkward, bulkier, and no less heavy. It is far too delicate to pack away. It must be carried along in the hands.

The shifting current pushed back and forth at the sides of the boat, and though the old outboard motor juddered along steadily behind them, Anna found herself wondering if they were even moving at all.

After some time she decided her best escape from the un-colored, unprogressing universe was simply to shut it out, and so she closed her eyes and tried to sleep. She was not terribly successful in the attempt—or perhaps she simply slept lightly and dreamt creeping dreams of a slow, noisy engine that hummed mournful doinas beneath the iron sea.

Soon, though, her mind began to wander, and she found it following the sounds of water and birds back to the wetlands of Poland.

It had been the first time her Swallow Man had taken her there, when she had still been very young. He had sat, his back against a long, thin tree, looking out into the blue sky, watching the birds call and wheel and dive into the water below the ridge.

"Look, Anna," he said, his voice bright with fondness. "There, standing, is a black stork. She only comes this far north in the summer. She is, of course, quite an elegant flier, but I prefer to imagine her walking up from Africa every year. Watch for her stately gait.

"There is the little wigeon duck, who never seems to worry.

"And there—a red-throated loon. Watch him fly. He looks as if he came to it by accident."

Of course Anna enjoyed learning the names and characters of all these birds, and it was clear to her that the Swallow Man loved them all very much. Where in Kraków she and Professor

Łania had been gladdened to see Monsieur Bouchard, here on the road the Swallow Man smiled to see the red-throated loon.

But try as she might, she could not find her way to loving these creatures the way that the Swallow Man did. Flying birds still made Anna feel nothing so much as loneliness.

She never thought about Kraków until she was lonely, and this was precisely the time when she most wished she could forget it.

"Swallow Man?" she said, and the Swallow Man said, "Yes."

"Do you never miss the city?"

The Swallow Man frowned. "I do."

Across the slope the black stork raised up its long-legged foot and then put it back down in indecision.

"I do, too," said Anna. "I miss the bells tolling the hour of the day. Sometimes I forgot that there was even such a thing as time, but then the bells would chime out and all of a sudden you knew that it was five o'clock."

The Swallow Man turned to look at Anna, and after a moment she saw an idea steal in through his eyes. With his long, delicate fingers, he plucked a thin pine needle from the heavy coat of them that the trees had dropped onto the ground, and with great care he sank it into a patch of sunlit earth at a very particular angle. Then, craning his neck to see the soft shadow it cast, he frowned and nodded gravely.

"Bong," he said in solemnity. "Bong. Bong."

It was a moment before Anna realized that this was not a word in an unfamiliar human language, but rather a very bad imitation of a clock-tower bell.

The Swallow Man allowed a tiny scrap of a smile in at the left corner of his mouth. "Actually," he said, "closer to three-fifteen."

Anna couldn't keep her smile down as well as the Swallow Man could, and she beamed up at him. "But how can you tell?"

The Swallow Man frowned and bobbed his head from side to side. "If you know true north and can estimate your latitude with some accuracy, it's no great feat to construct a rudimentary sundial. It's like a shadow clock. Look—the pine needle is the gnomon, and around it we imagine a clock face."

"What's a no-man?" asked Anna.

"The gnomon is the long, thin arm that points to the hour with its shadow. You see? Its name comes from Greek— 'knower,' because it knows the hour and tells us in its shadow language."

Anna nodded in understanding. "Oh," she said. "Like you."

The Swallow Man made a sound, once, quietly, like a laugh that had lost its way. "Huh."

Anna squished her face down low to the ground to look at the angled pine needle from the perspective of others like it.

Shortly she sat back on her knees and looked up at the Swallow Man.

"Swallow Man?" she said, and the Swallow Man said, "Yes."

"One day I would like to know everything, like you."

Now the Swallow Man frowned in earnest, and he sat in silent thought for so long that Anna thought he might not ever answer. Eventually, though, he took a quick breath in, as small and sharp as the tip of a pine needle, and he began to speak.

"I do not know everything, my dear," he said. "And I do not desire it, either. I cannot imagine it would be very pleasant. Knowledge is, of course, very important, because the things that we know become our tools, and without good tools at our disposal, it is quite difficult to remain alive in the world.

"But knowledge is also a kind of death. A question holds all the potential of the living universe within it. In the same way, a piece of knowledge is inert and infertile. Questions, Anna— questions are far more valuable than answers, and they do much less blowing up in your face as well. If you continue to seek questions, you cannot stray far off the proper road."

Anna did not understand. "Why?"

The Swallow Man smiled. "Well done."

If she had dozed, Anna woke; if she had only lain, she sat up. The old blue world passed out into the gray.

Again her eyes met the aged fisherman's, and he smiled at her.

Anna sighed and turned her eyes back to the sea.

More time had passed around her closed eyes, and, slowly, it had succeeded in wearing away at the thickness of the clouds, enough for the sun to cast a clean shadow down onto the surface of the water.

It was the shadow of spread wings.

Anna squinted up against the diffuse brightness, toward the sky. It was a variety of bird she had never encountered before, so large that it seemed as if it shouldn't fly. Like a guillemot's, its belly was white, but as it banked and turned on the wind, she saw the rest of it shine out in the sun, black as shadow—head, back, and wings. Anna's heart surged up to see it, as if her heart itself were a fishing bird, breaking through the surface of the still sea of her chest. Salt water stung her eyes. She wanted to yell out, to call to the bird in its own language, to cry and to hoot and to wave her arms, but before she could move, the bird tipped into the wind, circled, and sped off behind them.

The fisherman was smiling when Anna turned around to watch it disappear, but not because of the bird. His eyes were fixed over her shoulder.

"Look," he said in his funny accent, and Anna turned back.

There, shading the horizon, far off ahead, a grouping of islands had broken out of the eternity of gray. Anna was on her feet in a flash, craning out beyond the prow, eager to see what new, strange country they were headed for, but the fisherman spoke again.

"Cold water," he said. "Careful you don't fall in."

Anna wanted nothing less. She stood back, straight and tall, and looked out to the shore. There, hazy and indistinct, the great bulk of the land began to shade itself in behind the solidifying range of islands.

Yes. There it was.

It wasn't going away.

The tears that had threatened to tug open her eyes when the shadow of wings had passed above her began to fall now, cool and soft, like a rain that broke through all the pressure of heaven. No matter what she'd feared, no matter even what she had thought she knew for certain, there was still a something at the end of the water, a new land and a new language and perhaps even new kinds of birds that could wink silently down at her from out of the sky.

Across the surface of the water, Anna's shadow stood long and tall and sure, her head pointing straight to the coming country.

"What," said Anna, as much to herself as to the fisherman, "what is out there?"

# ACKNOWLEDGMENTS

My love and thanks are due very first and foremost to Livia Woods, scholar, traveling companion, midwife to my notions, and bang-up amateur pastry chef.

Thanks and apologies to Kate Broad, who took the first brunt of my reflexive inability to properly process criticism.

Thanks also to Alexandra Lee Hobaugh for early reading and tireless cheerleading; to my parents, Bob and Kathy Savit, who did me the ultimate compliment of reading the book aloud to one another; to Bethany Higa, whom I really ought to call more often; to Nat Bernstein, who read well, advised well, and pushed me out of the nest when I needed to go; and, of course, to John Rapson for his attention, his help, and his true and priceless friendship.

Oh, and Greg Jarrett, too, I guess.

I am indebted to Brent Wagner and his faculty for teaching me to be an adult and professional artist; I hope this may begin to alleviate the absence of many long-overdue thank-you notes.

Likewise, I would like to thank all the teachers and surrogate parents in my young life who saw me through when

I didn't necessarily deserve it. People like me don't get to places like this without you. Susan Hurwitz. Avi Soclof. Many, many others.

Immeasurable thanks to Catherine Drayton, who is a force of nature and who has changed my life. Thanks also to Lyndsey Blessing and all of my other InkWell champions, and to Kalah McCaffrey and Danny Yanez.

And, of course, great thanks to Erin Clarke, my editor and new friend; to her assistant, Kelly Delaney; to Erica Stahler, Stephanie Engel, Amy Schroeder, and Artie Bennett; and to the whole team at Knopf BFYR.

Thank you all!